Loman

FOSTER'S PRIDE BOOK 6

KATHI S. BARTON

This is a work of fiction. Names, characters, places, and incidents are products of the author's imagination or are used fictitiously and are not to be construed as real. Any resemblance to actual events, locations, organizations, or persons, living or dead, is entirely coincidental.

World Castle Publishing, LLC
Pensacola, Florida
Copyright © Kathi S. Barton 2023
Hardback ISBN: 9798379104245
Paperback ISBN: 9781960076366
eBook ISBN: 9781960076373
First Edition World Castle Publishing, LLC, February 27, 2023
http://www.worldcastlepublishing.com
Licensing Notes
Cover: Karen Fuller
Editor: Maxine Bringenberg

Prologue

Allen wished that he'd screened this call before he answered his phone. But he'd been counting the money that he'd be getting soon and forgot that he was avoiding bill collectors in addition to anyone else that called in. Mr. Foster was telling him things he didn't want to hear. Not that he thought that the man was right about his brother dropping out of the gallery show, but he knew when to talk and when to shut up about such matters.

Loman Foster, photographer extraordinaire, was his ticket to making a big windfall. Not that the kid would see much of it, but Allen didn't care about him. Once he got him to send him the pretty pictures he took, it would be a walk in the park for him to be a millionaire several times over. The kid was famous, and that was just what Allen needed. He remembered then that he was on the phone with his brother. Christ, didn't anyone care that he was a busy man? Apparently not.

"I have the contract right here. That's all I need to own that brother of yours if he doesn't come through like he said he would." The man, he thought he said his name was Keegan, asked him if it had been signed. "It's a verbal agreement that your brother and I have. He'll be bringing me photos, or you'll be holding the bag on this. I won't be messed around with on this. He said he'd bring them to me, and that's what I'm going to be holding him to."

Allen didn't know what that meant even to his own ears, and it bothered him that the man was laughing. While he didn't mind a good joke when it was about someone else, he couldn't stand the fact that this man was laughing at him.

"Where is that brother of yours anyway? I have a good mind to call him up right now and tell him how you're treating me. I don't care if you are his brother. I can tell you right now he won't care for the treatment I'm getting from you. This is a respectable gallery, and I won't allow him to back out of a good thing for the two of us. I hate to use a threat, but I'll ruin him if he doesn't come through like he said he would." Allen waved his daughter off when she simply barged into his office. He hated that she came into the office without so much as a knock. Keegan was talking, and he realized he had missed some of what he'd said. "What is it you're going on about?"

"I said that my brother has been trying to reach you for the last several weeks. Then when he leaves you a message, you call back at an ungodly hour and talk about how the show is going to be fantastic. You should go ahead and call him. He can tell you the same thing that—"

Andi reached over his phone and put it on speaker. Christ, there were times when he hated her. Like right now. She was talking to Keegan like she'd been speaking to him all along. After telling the man her name, she also told him she was the daughter of the asshole he'd been talking to. Keegan, or whatever his name was, told Andi that his brother wasn't going to be in the show.

"I can understand your hesitation, Mr. Foster. But we have spent a great deal of money advertising this showing for him. The least he could do is give us a good reason for not showing." Keegan told her that he'd found out from a good source that her father was skimming the sales for his own. Andi looked at her father. "I'm assuming that you have proof of this?"

"I do. Even if I didn't, it won't generate you much in the way of patrons out there when they hear it too. According to the things that I've heard from a very reliable source, he plans on ruining my brother by making sure that it's a terrible showing. That's a threat that I don't think your firm can stand by. You should ask your father, Ms. Allen, how much he's spent advertising for the show. I've been looking through all art and gallery magazines that I can think about, and there is not one mention of Loman's show coming up. Nor is there a word about it on the internet that I can find. Anywhere."

"I see." Andi asked Keegan if she could call him back. "I have to speak to my father about this. If what you say is true, and knowing my father the way I do, I don't doubt you. I'd say that your brother is right for pulling out. I'll give you a call back when I have more information to give you."

When the call was disconnected, he asked Andi why she'd said those things about him. She told him that they were true and that Loman was right in saying no. Allen stood up and then sat down. He hated that his daughters were taller than him by a good foot.

"How the hell do you know what I've done or not?" She told him that the checking account was overdrawn by thousands of dollars and that she had come here to talk to him about it. "So? Why do you think I'm pushing to have this showing so badly? You just ruined it all by sticking your nose in where it doesn't concern you. You're just like your sister and mother. You are Nosey as hell and not at all as smart as you think you are. Now I don't know that I'm going to be meeting payroll on time."

"Oh, but you will now, father. I found your banking information and took care that everyone gets paid. Imagine our surprise when there were several accounts with your name on them that you've been stashing cash in. Cash that didn't belong to you." Allen told her to put his money back. "I won't. And so you know, mother knows too. She's on her way in here now."

"You told your mother? Why would you do that to me? I'm your daddy, darling, and now you're going to be making trouble for me. Tell her that you were joking." Andi just sat there, and he heard his wife when she got off the elevator. "See that you take care of this, Andi. I won't have you ruining me when your mother thinks so highly of me. You know that she does too. Just the other day, we were talking about a second—" His wife came into the room. She looked like she could spit fire at him.

"Highly of you? Not on your life, you big overgrown moron. Christ, when I think about the things that I've had to do to keep this family in a home, all I want to do is hire someone to take you out." Meggie kissed Andi on the head, thanking her for giving her the information. Then she stared on him again. "Allen, we've been married for thirty-one years, and you've not changed one bit. Still out for a fast buck at someone else's expense. Well, you've gone too far this time. My father built this place up by having showings in his own home. And now look what you've done to it. We're reduced to having clients, good men and women that are trying to make a living out of their art leave us even before you've gotten around to taking all their money."

"It's just a little misunderstanding, Meggie. I would never take all their money." He had hoped that she'd not notice that he'd said not *all* of their money. But Andi did. She pointed it out to her mom. "Damn it. Why are you two even here today? I have things going on, and I want you two to get out of my office and leave me to my work."

"It *was* your office, Allen. Now it's mine and my daughters. We're taking over." Allen told her that she couldn't do that. "Of course, I can. And I am. Here is a copy of the paperwork you signed before we were married. Also, I'm thrilled to be able to tell you that I'm divorcing you. As of right now."

A thick file landed on the desk just as four men in security shirts entered *his* office. When they asked him how he wanted to be escorted out, he just stared at them. What the hell was going on with his wife and daughters today? There was no way that they could simply push him out of his job, one that he'd been doing for decades without any kind of trouble.

Once he was out on the sidewalk, after having been dragged to the elevator and then out of it. They had even dragged him through the lobby and out of the door before releasing him. He tried to get back into the building only to be told that if he entered again, he'd be arrested. Christ, this was a nightmare. He had things in his office that were stashed for him. Money being the biggest thing. Then he saw his other daughter coming toward him.

"Lindsley, your mother just tossed me out of the building like I've not been working there for most of my life." Lindsley just stared at him. "You have to get me inside. They're going to mess things up for the business, and what would your grandda say about that? He'd be livid. That's what he'd be. Get me inside, and I'll make sure that you have a job working with me for the rest of your life."

"How much will you pay me?" He asked her what she was talking about. "How much will you pay me for working for you for the rest of my life? I think that's a good question. Since you've never paid me for working for you when I was a child. How much, dad?"

"I've not thought about paying you at all. The business is heavily in debt, and people are already leaving because they found out that your mother is going to be in charge." She just stared at him. "What is wrong with you? You're acting like this isn't any of your problem. Well, it is. Who will pay your rent for you when I'm not working? Who is going to be able to get you the best gifts when Christmas rolls around? It's always me."

"First of all, I know that mom is divorcing you. I'm the one that talked her into it. Secondly, the business isn't in heavy debt because Andi found out where you were stashing money and took it all back so that the business could come out on top. Thirdly, and this one is one I think you should think about really hard, Dad, you're a thief. Not only that, but you're an asshole that hasn't paid any mind to any of us since you've been sponging off the gallery." Allen told her that she was ungrateful. "Am I? You've not a clue about anything about Andi and me. Nothing. Both of us have been out on our own for a very long time. I've been paying my own house payment for the last five years. I own my own car. Have adult credit cards as well as I haven't gotten anything from you for Christmas or my birthday in the last ten years. Andi either, for that matter."

"That would be your mother's fault. She never told me the dates or reminded me to send them to you." She pointed out that Christmas was the exact same time it was every year, December twenty-fifth. "I know when that is. I meant your birthday."

Lindsley reached for the door handle, and he moved closer to her to get in. Instead of opening the door for herself so he could sneak in, she told him to back off. He couldn't believe his own flesh and blood was treating him like this and told her that.

"It's only convenient for you to remember that we're related when you want something from me, isn't it? Is there anything else, dad? I mean, do you have anything else to tell me before I have you arrested for trespassing?" He told her that she was an ungrateful child. "To you, perhaps. But Andi and I are going to be taking care of the business with mom from now on, and you're going to be out on the streets. As it so happens, my job here is finished with you. I was told to delay you until the locks were changed on the house that you *used* to share with mom. Also, the car that brought you to work this morning is no longer anything that you're going to be able to use."

Allen was still standing there when he realized his daughter had gone into the building without him. He couldn't understand why they were all of a sudden treating him like this. Then he thought about the things that his wife and daughters had said to him over the course of the last few months.

He realized then that not only had they told him that he was going to be leaving the company, but now that he thought about it, they had even given him the date that he was going to be out on his ass. Damn it all to hell and back. Had he paid attention, he would have been able to put himself some cash away that he could get to so that he could ride out this shit storm that his wife was making for him. Allen wasn't worried about it, however. He knew that she'd be taking him back soon enough. She was just pissed off right now, and he'd be able to sweet talk her into letting him go back to the way things were before soon enough.

There wasn't any way that she'd be able to run

his company without him. Walking to a hotel, glad now that no one had bothered to take his company credit cards from him when he'd been given the boot. He's show them.

Right then, Allen decided to splurge on the best hotel he could go to and have room service bring him the finest steaks in the land. Waiting in line at the counter to get a room for the next few weeks, he was actually giddy with the prospect of hitting the business with a huge bill right now.

"My name is Allen Benson, and I'd like a room for the next week or so." The man told him the price, and he didn't even flinch at the ungodly amount of money that it was going to cost the gallery. "I'd also like to have dinner brought up to me as soon as possible. Steak and all the trimmings. And a bottle of the best wine you can find."

The man said nothing, but then Allen wasn't paying attention to him as he was thinking about his wife's face when she got the bill. As his credit card was handed back to him, he smiled at the clerk. Telling him to have a nice day.

"I'm sorry, sir, but your card has been denied.

Do you have another form of payment?" Allen pulled out the other cards that he had in his wallet, pissed off now that he'd been embarrassed because of his own family. Every card in his wallet was denied. "Do you have cash?"

"No, I don't have any cash on me. Christ, just send the bill to my office." The man simply lifted his nose at him. "I don't have time for you to be messing around with me today, buddy. Just charge the room and dinner to my business. You've done it before."

"I have, sir. But your wife called here last week and told us you'd be trying to do what you've done and said you're on your own. I didn't realize what she meant until your cards were denied. If you'd not mind, sir, I think that it's time that you were gone from here. We're a well thought of establishment, and riff-raff like you aren't the clientele we want here." He started to protest, but the man snapped his fingers, and three big men in security shirts showed up. "Now, as you've been told before, you can leave the easy way or the hard way. It's entirely up to you."

He left. Christ, what the hell was his family thinking when they took everything away from him.

He was going to make them pay when he got back in business. He wasn't going to forgive them for some time, either. Damned family. He wondered not for the first time why he'd even claimed them as his own.

~*~

Sarah worked the line of food alongside of her mate, Cass, while they served up Christmas dinner for the townspeople. She'd had a feeling that something was going to happen, but she just couldn't put her finger on what it was. Even reaching out to put her hands on some of the people in the room didn't make her feel any less anxious about her feelings.

"You should know that people are beginning to think you're pissed off at them. You have that look on your face that isn't all that friendly. I think you've even scared a couple of children with your look." Sarah looked at Cass and frowned. "I'm assuming this has something to do with what you were telling me about when we were home. That feeling you had of foreboding."

"Yes. Something is going to happen. I don't know if it's good or bad, but I just can't shake the feelings. It's more than likely nothing to worry about, but I can't shake that feeling." He asked her if he could help her. "Yes. Can you just gently reach out and see what you can find on what people are thinking about?"

He did just that. Telling her what each person was thinking as he went around the room as he continued to serve up the food with a smile. Sarah was ready to tell him to stop when he paused. Sarah asked him what was going on. He told her just to give him a second, and he'd tell her. Right now, he was getting more information to see what exactly was going on. With a glance, he nodded toward the doorway.

"See the three women that are over there by the door? The ones that are just sitting there and looking around?" She nodded. "They're the Benson women. The ones that Loman and the others were talking about last night that own the gallery that he wasn't going to be a part of when the mister was involved."

"Yes, they have the gallery that he's thinking about helping out because they've fired the dad or something. What's going on?" He asked if he told her if she would do as he asked. "I think you know the answer to that even before you asked me. What's going on?"

"Mr. Benson is here as well. He is not in the building, but he's close enough to being around that they're a little afraid to leave the building, with good reason. While they don't think he'll hurt anyone else around, they're afraid that if they go out the door, he'll cause trouble, and someone will get hurt. He's upset that they have taken away his money maker. They don't want anything to happen to anyone here. They're very afraid that he'll ruin the day for a great many people here." She asked him if he knew where Mr. Benson was. "No, not yet. I don't know him well enough to know his mind. I can only assume that he's close like they fear he is. Since you won't go someplace safe, tell me what you're thinking about doing to keep this from being messy."

"I say that we go over there and talk to the women. Then we see what they want to do. We could, I suppose, take care of it right now by having Parker go and mess him up, but that won't solve their issue down the line. Correct?" He said he liked the idea of Parker taking care of him, but she was right. "I'm forever right, Cass. Haven't you figured that out by now?"

"I must have forgotten myself for a moment.

All right, you head over there and see what you can find out. I'm going to go outside and see if I can feel anything there. Please be careful, love. I don't want anything to happen to you." She kissed him on the mouth and made her way to the women.

As soon as she was close enough to them, she could tell they were indeed terrified. Not just of whatever was going on with Allen but at getting anyone in here hurt like Cass had told her. Sitting down with them, Sarah introduced herself to the three of them.

"Also, I have a bit of magic that I've been using since we got here today. I'm assuming that you're aware that we're all lions." Meggie introduced herself to her and her daughters, saying she had just found that out when she'd overheard someone talking about it. "Good. Do you know where Allen is? I mean, any idea where I can send my husband and the others to keep you guys safe?"

"We saw him when we first arrived. None of us have seen him in town before we left, but he must have figured on coming here to talk to Loman himself. I don't know what he thinks he could say to him, but that's all we can think of right now. I don't want your brother to be hurt by anything he says. Just don't believe a word that comes out of his mouth. Please?" Sarah asked if they thought he was dangerous. "Only to himself, we think. But then, I never expected him to rob other people for their sales either. I'd like to tell you that he's not the man I married, but he's exactly the man that I married. But I'm taking care of that as we speak."

"We'll take care of him if you're all right with that." She nodded, as did her daughters. "All right. I'm going to send the others out to find him. To either have him move along or be arrested if he's so much as spitting on the sidewalk." The three of them laughed. "Good, you've not lost your complete sense of humor. All right. Give me a second, and I'll see what I can figure out."

Sarah didn't leave them, but she did make sure that the others in the building knew what was going on. As soon as Ronan and Loman went out to where Cass was, she felt a good deal better about her mate going outside to take on a moron.

As soon as Ronan came back in, she thought that something had happened to Cass. Then when he joined his brothers behind the line again, she told the women that she was going to find out what had happened. Before she could get up and find her mate, he sat down next to her.

"He's been arrested. Just now." Cass kissed her on the mouth and smiled at the women after introducing himself. The women were concerned about why he'd been arrested, and Cass laughed. "He was standing next to a Christmas display in town, in one of the shops and decided that he was going to mess it up. I haven't any idea why he thought that was going to be a good idea, but he tore it down and kicked the broken pieces into the street. As he was just about to start the mess on fire, the police caught him in the act and took him in. Donnelly, one of the officers there, said that he'd make sure that he was in a cell until after New Year's. That's when the shop owner is planning to come back from their vacation. They'll hold him until they find out if they want to press charges or not."

"Oh, thank goodness that no one was hurt. I've been worried about what he'd do when he got desperate." Meggie looked at her daughters. "Andi said I should press charges against him for running us off the road on the way here."

"You should. For no other reason than to keep him out of your hair while you're here." Cass said that he'd make sure that the police talked to them before they left here today. "I'm glad that you allowed us to be helpful in this. If you're hungry, there is plenty to eat. We're just waiting on the last group of officers to come in and eat with their families. Then people will begin to gather up the leftovers they want to take home, and we'll start the cleanup. We're going to start doing this every year for Thanksgiving and Christmas. It's worked out very well for everyone."

The three of them decided they'd eat but insisted on helping them clean up when they were finished. Telling them they'd appreciate their help, the family got themselves plates of food and sat back down. Sarah made her way to the back room to begin the clean-up back there as the line was taken care of for now. However, there were already a group of men and women there washing up the pans they'd used to serve.

It was well past seven when they were finishing up. Even the Benson women looked like they were having a good time cleaning up the tables. As they were storing away the tables for another time, Loman came out of the room in the back and began taking the trash out. Meggie helped him.

"Do you suppose he's the mate to one of them?" Sarah looked up at Cass when he asked her that. "I mean, he's the last one of us to be mated, so it stands to reason they might be. I think it would be good for Loman to have someone in his life. He's such a loner."

"I didn't even think of that. How do we tell? It seems to me that everyone else knew that we were mates before you did. Is there some kind of tell?" Cass told her that her best bet was to ask him when he came back in. "You're thinking that it's the mom?"

"No, I mean, I don't know, but if she's not, then he'll have a feeling about her, a protection feeling that will tell him that she's close to someone that he's mated to." Sarah nodded and kept an eye out for Loman and Meggie to come back in. However, if she was looking for a tell, she was disappointed when he came in by himself and walked right by the daughters.

For the rest of the evening, she thought about things she wanted to talk to Loman about. He was going to be staying with her and Cass until his furnace was finished being put in, and she was happy about that. As they were watching a Christmas special on the television, just the three of them, Sarah, just asked him if they were his mate.

"Are you thinking I'm man enough to handle both of them?" She was embarrassed, and he continued to tease her about it. Finally, he shook his head. "I don't think so. I didn't really get all that close to either one of them, but the mom, and she's not my mate. However, I do like them. Meggie was talking to me about the things that are going to happen at the gallery when it's closed down, and I think I'm going to help them out like I've been talking about for a few days. It's a win-win for them and me, I think. I think too that it might be a good relationship with us and them for a while as well."

"I'm glad to hear that. I'm sort of disappointed that they're not your mate. I liked the three of them and could see they'd fit well in our little group." He said they could still fit in. "Yes, I suppose, but having them as sisters would have been much nicer. Don't you think?"

"Yes. But as I said, I didn't get close to the

daughters, so it might still be a good thing for you. Because, as you know, me having a mate is all about you, my dear sister." She smacked him on the shoulder, and he laughed. "I've been traveling for a while to be here, so I think I'm going to go up to bed. Mom wants me to remind you guys that tomorrow morning she is coming here for breakfast. Something about you owing her bacon and eggs."

After Loman left them, she asked him what that was supposed to mean. Laughing, Cass told her that his mom had a bet with him. About how long the cherry pies would last from the moment they opened today. Then for him to tell her who got the last piece.

"There weren't any cherry pies left over there." Cass said there had been eight of them, but as soon as they'd been sliced, they disappeared. "Disappeared? Or did your brothers eat them all? I can't see that many pieces of pie go so quickly. However, that's not what happened at all."

"It was Ronan, wasn't it? He was responsible for three of the pies being gone. He was asked to take some of them over to the nursing home for those who couldn't get here today. There were dinners too that went with him, so that leaves five. Loman and myself took two more of them to the police station. After that, we've no idea what happened to the other three pies. The best we can figure is that people saw them being laid out and snatched them right up. I didn't get a slice of any of them. Shit head. I'm going to make him pay for that."

"So what does that have to do with the bet you lost to your mom? Not that I care, but I'd like some details." He told her what the bet was about. "You bet your mom that you'd be able to find the other pies, and you didn't? That's why you owe her breakfast?"

"Yes. It was funny too. I kept an eye on those pies all afternoon, and I never once saw anyone take a single slice of them. There was plenty of pumpkin and apple left but nothing of the cherries." She smiled at him. "You know what happened to them, don't you?"

"I do. And you shouldn't have to cook for your mom since she cheated." Cass asked what she was talking about. "They're here. She had me bring the last two pies here before they were sliced. And I wasn't to tell anyone that we had them. Your mom wanted to win, so she had me take the pies out of the building and bring them here so she could have them, what she told me anyway was that she wanted a slice tomorrow."

"I'll be damned. My mom cheated." Sarah laughed along with Cass as he went on about how his sainted mother had cheated him out of breakfast. "What are you going to do with the pies now that you know it was a scam?"

"I'm going to have a piece. How about you?" The two of them enjoyed two slices each of the pie with ice cream and whipped cream because they could. It was a great dessert, especially since she knew that it was part of a plan to get back at Cass. Tomorrow he was going to make his mom confess to what she'd done, and it was going to be funny for her to be a part of it. Who knew that Camilla had a dishonest bone in her body?

When they made their way up to their room, she thought perhaps this was the best tradition she'd ever been a part of. Feeding families and being around them at such a time was not just fun, but it was fulfilling too. Even as she got into bed, she thought that long after this year, she was going to keep up with helping the community like this and have their own children be a part of it as well, just as she'd told the Benson women.

Things like this it was what made people more willing to help others when it was needed. Yes, Sarah thought, this is what people needed to make them all feel welcome and a part of something.

Chapter 1

Loman didn't move from his position when the momma giraffe and her calf joined the tower or group of them he'd been photographing for the last hour. He was magnificent, even being as small as he was at about six feet. He couldn't have been any more than a few days old. As they began enjoying the last of the grasses on the ground, he snapped several more pictures as his brother contacted him.

"I'm sorry to bother you." Loman said it was fine. He was just about finished anyway. Ronan said that he had some information for him on his home. *"Good. I only have a few more days here, and then I'm coming home*

for a while. I'm taking a month off to get my house in shape."

"Your furnace is finally installed. Correctly this time, and I've also had the roof checked out, as well as the rest of the house for you. The inspector said that you'd have a few more years on the one that is there. Five at the most. So I hope you don't mind, but I went ahead and had it replaced completely while no one is in residence." Loman thanked him and told him that he really appreciated him looking out for him. *"No worries. The kitchen looks fantastic. I love the way that Brook's crew tore out all the existing walls and put in more electrical outlets. It's worked out good for us in all the rooms."*

"She said that it does make it easier for when you have a lot of shit to plug in." Loman noticed the pack of lionesses making their way to the tower. *"I might have to cut you off here, Ronan. I have a situation here that might cause me to have to take off soon."*

He told his older brother what was going on. If he was right, they'd go after the calf by separating him from his mother and the others. The tower would try and save the little one, but they were hungry. The calf wouldn't be able to keep up with others if they ran either.

"You're not allowed to interfere, are you?" He said that he'd rather not. Not unless they came too close to where he was. *"I would imagine if you were to just happen to shift, they'd feel the presence of a larger lion and take off, Right?"*

"Not females. They'd only feel that I was some jerky lion trying to take their food. One of the lionesses has given birth recently. I'm not sure if she still has cubs to feed or not, but I'm not going to get involved in their fight. Have you not seen your own females fight with each other until some idiot comes in, mostly you, to try and break it up? What happens, Ronan?" He told him that they turned on him as a pride. "Right. And if it's all the same to you, I'd just as soon keep all my fur where it — Later, brother."

Loman left his camera on the tripod and set it to take pictures every ten seconds. It would be worth the camera getting destroyed if for no other reason than the shots he'd get. Moving back deeper into the little bit of overgrowth he had found, he made sure he was as covered as he could be. Loman allowed just enough of his lion to go so they'd think he had already passed through.

The sounds behind him were terrifying. He

knew the exact moment that the lionesses attacked and how the tower was protecting the little one. The sound of their deadly kick to the lions was loud, and the cries of the injured made his own lion curl a little tighter to him. When the fight took off, running away from him rather than toward him, he sat there for several minutes, waiting to not hear anything more from the bloodshed.

Loman studied the scene. Blood was everywhere. While he couldn't see the animals anymore, there was enough blood surrounding the trees that he knew one of them had been hurt enough that they'd be dead soon, if not already. Picking up his camera, he was glad to see that it hadn't been broken. He went back through the pictures to see what had happened.

"*I can feel your anger. Are you all right? Do I need to pop over there and take care of things for you? I will, you know that, don't you?*" He told Parker what had just happened. "*Oh, I'm sorry, Loman. That must have been heartbreaking for you. You said he was only a few days old? But I guess I can understand why you don't interfere. I'm not sure that I could be so brave. But then, it's like my magic. To interfere means that it comes back on your tenfold. But that's not why I contacted you. Other than your anger. When will you be home again? No rush, but I was thinking that you need to come home and see the gallery they're working on. It's coming along much better and faster than I thought it would. Brook has the best workers, I think."*

"I have another assignment here, then I'll have to work on getting them developed and sent out. The second set of pictures that I'm taking are of some waterways. I'm not sure what they want, but I'm actually a week early in going there, so I'm going to leave tonight." She asked him if he was all right. *"Yes. Physically I am. Mentally? I'm not sure. I need a conversation with Jasper."*

"Jasper? Are you getting magic, Loman? You never did check out if either of the Benson sisters were your mates. Could that be it?" He asked her to stop pushing them at him. *"I'm not pushing them at — okay, so I am. I think that everyone is. We want you to be happy."* He felt his anger toward his family, something that he never thought he'd have flare up again.

"What makes you think that I'm not happy already? I'm not hurting anyone with what I do, am I? No, I'm not. I come home when I have to. Here lately, not as much, but I do when I have to. I work hard. Christ." He thought about

his anger toward this woman and didn't care what she did to him. *"Why is it that everyone wants me to be mated? I have no problem with it when it happens in the natural course of things. But now I'm not wanting to come home because I know that you or one of the others is going to try to set me up with someone, and that's not how it works. At least not how I want it to work. Damn it."*

"I'm sorry." He could feel her anger toward him, and he, again, didn't care right now. He was pissed off too. Loman wanted them to just leave him the fuck alone. *"I will drop it and leave you alone. We all will if that's what you want."*

"Now you're going to be petty." She didn't say anything more to him but appeared in the country that he was in, right before him. And she didn't look happy either. "You're going to threaten me, Parker? Tell me, if I don't come home with you, that you're going to make it so that I'm not in contact with my family? I'm not like the rest of you. Not one bit. I live alone. I work alone. It's terrifying for me to think that there is a woman out there that is going to be like you all are and expect me to be this chatterbox all the time. To woo her in some way. That's not me. At all."

"I know that, you moron. But there are things going on at home that you…Do you want me to tell you, or do you want to just stay out here and let yourself be alone without a mate?" He asked her what was going on. "It'll make you want to come home. I'm not sure I could handle feeling like I've blackmailed you by telling you something that you'll resent me for the rest of my life. I love you, Loman."

"What's going on? And before you tell me, you should know I love you too. I'm frustrated. Pissed off and not feeling myself." She looked at him then, and he could tell she knew something was wrong with him. Loman was glad it wasn't just him who thought he was off his meddle. "What is it you see, Parker? Something is off about me, and I'm not—"

For the fourth time today, he leaned over and threw up. It was mostly bile and water now, but he was really feeling something was wrong. He didn't think that he was sick. He couldn't get sick. However, when warm arms wrapped around him, he felt himself being laid down.

Loman asked for his mom. He saw her for a second before everything seemed to dim out for him.

He could hear voices but not see or understand what they were saying to him. Then there was Jasper.

"You see me?" He nodded his head and said that he hurt. "You do. Very much so. I can heal you, my dear brother, but you're going to hurt more before you are better. The blood I gave you long ago has been poisoned with iron."

"I have iron-poor blood?" Loman giggled. Or he thought he did. "Something is wrong with me, Jasper. Please fix me. I don't want to die."

"You won't, my friend." He must have passed out but did wake to the feeling that he had to throw up again and again. Parker and a beautiful woman were standing over him at some point, but he couldn't lift his arm to touch her.

He didn't know what was going on or even if the dreams or whatever they were were really happening. Loman was going to die, and he just knew it. Something was wrong, and no one but Jasper was able to fix him. He didn't want him to die either and said that. The voice that answered him, if it was a voice and not more dreams, told him that Jasper was going to be just fine as was he. Loman certainly hoped so.

~*~

Lindsley watched the man sleep. It wasn't as fitful as it had been. He just looked like he was resting peacefully. She leaned back in the chair that had been brought into the room when Loman was first brought here. Lindsley didn't think she'd ever forget how he looked when she was asked to help hold him down eleven days ago.

"He has been poisoned with iron. Not as much as it would have taken to fell a man like him, but with the combination of his lion being ill too, it's made him near to the point of a comatose state." Lindsley had asked Ronan who and how it had happened. "I don't know. Parker is looking into it. To see if she can trace the iron to someone. But we have to get it out of him. It's shutting down his organs, and he'll have to be on life support forever. He's an immortal, you know."

She did. So were her sister and mother. Her dad? Well, right now, she could care less what happened to him. Yes, he was her dad, but he'd been a fucking prick to them since she could remember. He'd even taken money from her bank account just after setting it up with money from her birthday.

While she'd been holding him down, something

that she thought would be fairly easy as he was so ill, she'd been knocked back against the wall at one point. It had been bad enough that her head was bleeding, and her right shoulder had been broken. Almost as soon as she stood up to have someone take her to the emergency department, it was all healed. Even the blood from her head wound seemed to absorb right back into her body. No one said a word about it. Even to this day, she hadn't been asked about it.

She brushed a stray lock of hair from Loman's brow, then leaned back in her chair. "I think that I'm your mate. I don't know for sure, as I'm not talking about it to anyone. But my sister Andi and I have been each other's confidants for years now. Since we were children." She had no idea why she was talking to Loman, but it felt right to her. "The iron that they took out of you, a great deal I was told, is being traced right now."

Parker told her that she could tell him things if she wanted. That he may well hear her voice. When she sat up in the chair, she made her way to the window that looked out over the back yard. She knew this was his home. Her sister and mother had been staying here since he came here. It was about the nicest house she'd been in, even counting her own home.

"My father shot my mom. The day he'd been released from jail. We thought for sure that she was going to die. It was touch and go there for a while, but she's better now. Thanks to your magical family." There were flowers starting to bloom in the rose garden behind his house. "She's still in the hospital. Andi and I, along with your family, take turns going there to sit with her then the other comes here. Andi reads to you. She thinks that if she does that, you'll be considerably smarter when you wake up. However, your mom told us that you were brilliant. Of course, I didn't know what she meant by that until she showed me her collection of newspaper articles about how you graduated from college at fifteen with an art history degree. Also, she said that you're an attorney for yourself."

"I wanted to be able to read over contracts that I get so that I don't get into a deal that my ass can't cover." She turned to look at Loman when he spoke to her. "I don't know your name. Do I?"

"Lindsley Benson. My father is Allen. The one that tried to shaft you." He asked her if she'd come and hold his hand. "I've been doing that a great deal. It somewhat comforting to me. I didn't know that you'd mind all that much."

"Yes. I'm afraid to move, to be honest with you. I can feel my muscles tightening up in pain when I wiggle my toes." When she took her seat again, Lindsley reached for his hand. "I've been a bastard for the last—I don't know how long I have been. But I was particularly mean to Parker. I was happy to wake up just now as my regular self. I thought she'd turn me into something."

"She told us all. That it was the iron that was making you not yourself. Also, I guess there was enough magic that had been given to you with it that turned you. I think she called it inside out. That your personality changed so much that you didn't know how to deal with it. So anger was what you used." He told her he was sorry if he'd said anything to her to hurt her. "It's fine. You're calm now, and I'm betting I'm seeing the real Loman Foster."

She watched him doze off and on. When he woke, Loman would ask her questions or ask for something. He was concerned about his camera and his pack. Also, he wanted to have something to drink. Giving him the ice chips that were forever in the cup seemed to satisfy him immensely.

Lindsley let the rest of the family know he was awake, and talking was easy enough. Parker or one of the others had given her the magic to do so. They said that they would come over a few at a time so as not to overwhelm him. She had heard that Loman preferred his own company to that of a large crowd.

When her cell phone went off, she saw it was her father again. Turning off the call, she let it go to voice mail. As it was right now, Lindsley wasn't sure there was any more room for him to leave any messages. He'd been calling her for days now and begging her to let him into the offices again. There was no way. When Loman woke this time, he stared at her for a few seconds before he spoke again.

"You said your dad shot your mother. Why did he do that?" She told him what her father had said. "Did he really think that having her dead would get him back to the way things were? Christ, I don't understand humans at all. No offense on that. You seem normal."

They both laughed, and he dozed off again. This time when he woke, it was as if he'd never stopped talking to each other. He asked her if they'd locked him out of the offices before he could get things squared away for himself.

"Absolutely. Even though we gave him notice about a month before we came in and kicked him to the curb, he didn't do anything. Andi told us that he'd not. Thinking that we were just trying to scare him. It was funny, really. We found the money that he had stashed all over his office. Credit cards that were taken out for the company. Most of them were maxed out, but mom is making arrangements to have them paid off." He asked about passports. "Just one in his name. I don't know how he thought that was going to work for him. I mean, he's been watched for the last month of his being there."

"He seems like a man that isn't stable." She said that he was obsessed with running the business and ruining it for himself. "I don't know him, but it's doubtful that he thinks that he'll ruin it. It's his money maker, and he would have kept it running even if he had to bring in people like me, who he would bully into putting their art in the gallery. If he used his tactics like he did on me to fifty people, and only five weren't savvy enough to know that they didn't have to conform to his rules, then he'd keep it running. I can see a few of the artists that I know who wouldn't have said anything to the police because their self-esteem would have been taken down a notch or two."

"You know, I think you're right." He smiled and closed his eyes. She could tell that he was still awake. "They told me that I have magic too. That it will only get stronger if I bond with you. I had to ask what that meant. I'm not ready to jump into bed with you, however."

He laughed before speaking. "To be honest with you, Lindsley, I don't think I could do much more than hold you. I'm exhausted and hurting. Not as much as I had been before you held my hand, but I don't want to move. Not yet, at any rate."

"How do you even know that I'm your mate? You know it could be Andi, and I'm just getting magic because I've been hanging around with your family. Who I like, by the way." He said he liked them as well, but she could prove it to them both by smelling his neck. "Sure, I'm going to lean into your bed to smell you—you do know that you've been lying here for the last week and a half without so much as a sponge bath. There is no telling how long before that you were without a shower. You'll just smell like body odor, won't you?"

"I have no idea. If I'm thinking right, it's been nearly three weeks since I've had a shower. It's important to my job that I don't smell fresh. Do you know what I mean?" She said that she did. Surprising herself with her answer. "I don't know what I'd smell like to you, but I can smell you, and your scent calls to me. You smell of earth, rich soil and flowers. Like nature to me. Fresh in the spring. Winter, too with all the snow."

"That's very romantic." She didn't want to know for sure, but there were things she'd been unable to ask people about since she'd been sitting with him. Leaning into his throat, she moaned when the scents hit her system. Not only did he smell of earth, but not like body odor like she'd thought. It was as if he was the blues and greens of the field for her. Fresh apples being sliced for a pie. Dizzy, she had to sit back down.

"You're my mate."

"I'm glad." When he went to sleep this time, she let go of his hand to pace the room. While she wasn't a pacer usually, the things she'd figured out in the last few seconds were making her have even more questions. It wasn't until Sarah came into the room that she felt as if she was going to bust if she didn't talk to someone. "He's my mate."

"I know. How do you feel about that?" She told Sarah that she wasn't entirely sure just now. "That's understandable. It's all new to you. By the way, I've been helping out with some of the background checks on your employees, and I have a list of them that need to be gotten rid of. One of them was having an affair with your father. He's a piece of work, isn't he?"

"He is. I knew about the affair. I think that was what set my mom off on this mission of hers to ruin him. He nearly did that to her." Sarah sat down and watched her at the window now. "I don't know what I'm supposed to do now. I mean, what, if anything, can I do to make him feel better."

"Nothing right now. He just needs to rest. The two of you are going to be fine. It will take some adjustments in both of your lives, but you'll be happy. I think happier than any of us right now." She told Sarah that she thought they were busting with happiness. "We are. So think how happy you're going to be when you two are together."

"The magic that was given to him by Jasper this time, I was told it was quite a bit. Like enough to make him partly fae. I don't think I ever believed in other creatures before this. I mean, I knew there were shifters in our business, but so long as they didn't have any trouble, I didn't either. They were just people." Sarah told her that most of the people that she had working for her were shifters. "I thought as much. They're very strong. I've always marveled at how easily they could pick up art pieces without so much as breaking a sweat."

Lindsley just nodded when Sarah didn't say anything more. There were all kinds of questions going through her head, and not one of them would slow enough that she could figure out a way to talk to her.

"You know, I can read your mind, right?" Lindsley asked her if she could fix it so that she was calm in her mind. "I can. Then I can do a nice little walkthrough and answer things that I can. Carmella would be the one to talk to about some things. She's a wonderful woman."

"Yes, she's been so helpful to me on a great many things." Finally sitting down, she took Loman's hand into hers. "When I'm near him, I feel like I can do whatever I set my mind to. Then when I'm with my mom, all I can think about is him. I think that's why Andi has been staying longer with our mom. She knows more than I do about this."

They talked about the things that were in her mind. After a time, she was able to calm her mind down enough that she could figure out things on her own. Loman slept the entire time, and she was glad he was getting some much-needed rest. Lindsley couldn't wait for him to be able to get up and get moving.

At dinner time, she was able to get him to sit up in a chair. He was weak, he told her but felt better sitting up. He didn't feel so bedridden. Laughing while he moved to the chair, she was glad for the help when not just Ronan showed up but Brook as well. They brought them all food and some egg drop soup for Loman. It was about all he could handle just now.

Once they got him back in bed, he was awake more. Sitting up made him a little tired and sore, but he was able to hold whole conversations with everyone without slipping into a nap. Once they were all gone, leaving behind some juice for them both. Loman asked her if she'd sleep with him.

"No sex. Even the thought of trying to satisfy you makes me hard. I'm not that strong yet. But I would enjoy having you by my side." She pulled off her shirt and pants and used one of his shirts for a nightgown. Getting into bed with him, she was glad when he wrapped his body around hers.

Not being as active as she normally would be at home and work, she wasn't as tired as she thought she should have been. Loman didn't snore at all, and his breath on her shoulder, even through his shirt, was comforting to her.

Tomorrow she was going to have to go to the gallery. Things were going on there that she needed to be on top of. Then she was going to see about her father and what his fate was. He'd been arrested on attempted murder charges as well as the things that he'd pulled at the gallery.

Cass told her that her father was facing some serious prison time for the mail fraud of sending money overseas as well as not paying artists that had had a showing in their gallery. Tens of millions of dollars had been found stashed away in different accounts. Lucky for them, Andi was able to run it all down and get it back to the places that it belonged. The only thing worrying them now was the credit cards and paying for advertising for their grand opening.

"You're thinking too hard." Rolling to her side, she looked up at Loman when he spoke. "You're very tense right now. Want to talk to me about things? I'm sure I can help you with some of your thoughts. Like money."

"We're just barely making it." He said he'd help them out. "You don't have to do that, Loman. We'll get it taken care of."

"You're my mate. Your sister is now my sister, and your mother is my family as well. When we need help, I'm going to help. I have a bit of money. Quite a bit, as a matter of fact. And if there isn't enough from my accounts, I'll ask my family—who is also your family to help out. They will. Simply because I've fallen in love with you." She wasn't sure what to say. Loman kissed her on the nose. "Go to sleep. It's late, and tomorrow, we'll have a serious conversation about the needs of the gallery."

She didn't know why but she believed him. Rolling back to her side again, she closed her eyes. In seconds she felt her body begin to relax and her mind calm. Before slipping away, she felt Loman kiss her on the ear and him telling her that he loved her. It was too late for her to say the same to him. It was like a plug had been pulled out of her, and she was falling into a void of sleep.

Chapter 2

Loman didn't like using a cane, but his brother told him that he needed to be stronger before he could shift and be back to his normal self. Locking himself in his dark room, he began working on the photos that he had taken before being brought home. He was really proud of his work on this one and decided that even though it was bloody as hell, he was going to include the calf being killed by the lion pride. If the magazine that he was working for didn't want them, he was going to put them with the other pictures that he'd taken and put them in another book.

So far, Loman had nineteen books—called

tabletop books—to his name right now. Not his real name. He only put L.F. on them. But each of the pictures was signed by his small signature of a paw. He wondered if anyone had ever figured out that it was the paw print of a kitten he'd found when he'd been first on the job. Smiling at the thought, he was surprised when someone rang the doorbell on his dark room.

"I can't open the door right now." It was Andi. She wanted to know if she could stay for dinner. "Of course, you can. You can live here too, and that would make me happy. I'm in the process of developing some of the photos that I took while out. I'll be ready to open the door in about an hour. Then we'll have a nice dinner. Lindsley is at the gallery. So it'll just be the two of us."

"Great. If you're serious about me moving in here, I'd be thrilled. I have a home, but I've just come to the realization that it's not really a home but a house. It's not very fulfilling. Not like I get when I'm around your entire clan." He told her that they were a pride. "Yes, I knew that I think. All right. Which room can I take over?"

"Anyone you want. I've not been around up there very much since I've been home. So you'll have to figure it out on your own." Andi said she could do that. "Oh, I almost forgot. There are several messages for you that came into the house. I don't know what they're about, but they're on my desk."

After thanking him, she said she'd get to them. As he began to develop the rest of the pictures, he was saddened by what he was seeing. But as Parker told him, it was the way that things worked. While he was waiting on the bath to do its job, he thought of the first time he'd taken pictures.

He'd been eight years old. His family had been at a wedding, and someone had left a camera on one of the tables. Loman hadn't tried to steal it, though the man later accused him of it. He had watched the camera just sit there for several hours. Then when no one had picked it up, he did so and started taking pictures with it. Thinking at the time that someone should have been taking pictures all along with it.

The wedding was for a human couple — not that it mattered. They'd been friends of his mother's, that had invited them all to celebrate their day with them. Glad to have something to do, Loman had gone around the room, snapping pictures. Even going as far as directing some of the shots that he wanted and had even taken the bride and groom outside so that he could get some lovely shots of them in the colorful fall trees.

Loman knew that they were humoring him about the pictures. He was all right with that too. It had been something to do at first, but once he started taking them, it felt like something he'd been called to do. Something that he enjoyed. However, when they realized the photographer they hired had been drinking and was in a stupor in a corner, they were very upset with him. It wasn't until they developed the film and saw the pictures that they came to see him and his mother.

"Have you seen these?" Lily, the bride, had laid them, all ninety pictures that had been taken that day in front of his mother. "These were supposed to be memories of our special day. Something that we can't do again and just look at them."

Mom picked them up and handed them, one at a time to him. He knew that he was going to be in deep trouble. The shots were blurry. Some of them were of the ground. There were pictures of the cake off-center a bit and looking like it was falling over. There were several pictures of the ceremony itself, too, ones that he knew for certain that he'd not taken. But he didn't open his mouth. The woman and her husband were pissed off enough.

When the pictures his mother handed him suddenly looked clear, he knew they were the ones he'd taken. Even then, he kept his mouth closed while thinking that he'd not done such a terrible job. The one of the bride and groom out in the woods was beautiful. The sun streaming down through the trees hit them perfectly in the face, just as he had wanted. No one said a word as they went through all the shots of the day. As the last photo was handed to him, he laid it carefully on the pile and looked at his mom.

"You've no idea how sorry I am that this happened, Lily." She nodded, staring at him as if she wanted a hole in his head. "We'll pay you back for the photos. I'm not sure what we can do to replace your pictures, but Loman and I, we'll repay you for what has happened here."

"The ones on the top are the ones that were taken

by the photographer that we hired, Carmilla. The man that we paid good money to take our wedding pictures." Mom glanced at him and then asked Lily what she'd said. "Loman took the ones that are of good quality. The ones were…I have no words to say how spectacular his photos are. Nor do I know how to thank him for…without Loman picking up the camera and taking those shots for us, we wouldn't have had any kinds of memories of the day. Not a one. These are better than we could have had if the man we did hire hadn't been drunk on his butt. Loman saved the day for us, Carmilla. And we want to thank you both from the bottom of our hearts."

"I didn't steal the camera, Ms. Lily." She said that the other man, Mark Henson, was blaming Loman for being a thief and for taking credit for his work. "He's seen these?"

"Oh yes. When we got the pictures back yesterday, imagine our surprise when he only gave us the ones I knew you'd taken. Of course, I didn't know when you were taking them that you actually had film in the camera. But I did remember the ones you'd taken outside." Her new husband, Paul, cleared his throat before speaking.

"You waited on the sun to set just right before you let us move. I thought that you were having fun with us, watching us hold onto one another for a bit too long. But I enjoyed holding my new wife, or I might—you waited on the sun to be in the perfect place before you snapped it, didn't you, young man?" Loman had nodded, telling him that it wasn't as bright because he wanted it to come through the trees before touching their faces. "When I saw that picture, I knew with a certainty that you took it. And that you, with the right encouragement, would continue to get better and better at taking pictures the older you got."

The wrapped gift was put on the table. He didn't touch it even though the couple had said it was for him but waited until his mom said it was all right to open. Once he got the camera, a very nice camera, out of the box, he told Mr. Paul that he couldn't accept it. It was much too expensive for a gift. It was Ms. Lily that got down on her knees in front of him to tell him what he should do.

"Without you, Loman, we'd have nothing. As it is right now, we have the most amazing memories of any wedding ever taken. You captured moments in the day, not people just milling about. There are pictures of my parents there that caught them in the perfect light—they're smiling at one another, and I can almost touch their love. Photos of the children having fun out in the yard with the leaves. No one would have gotten those for us. You didn't pose us but the one time to get shots of us. As I said, you captured memories for us, not just pictures." To this day, he still feels his face heat up when he thinks of the kiss she'd given his cheek. "We want you to have this camera to make a name for yourself. Get out there and continue doing what you have a gift for. Please. For us. Someday we want to be able to look in a magazine and say, 'Hey, we know that man. He took our wedding pictures when he was just a little boy.'"

He'd done just what they wanted him to do. With the encouragement of his parents, then his grandparent after his father had passed away, Loman had gone out and made not just a name for himself, but he'd made a good deal of money. Taken photos of animals and things that no one else would dare do. And now, here he was, living in a nice home with a mate and her family, doing what, as he'd been told, he meant to do.

After the last picture was hung up to dry, he made his way to the other baths and began cleaning up. When he was finished up, leaving things as clean as they were when he came in, he moved to the door and unlocked it. He was surprised to find not just Andi there but her mom as well. He asked what had happened.

"Nothing. We just wanted to give you an update on — why do men always think that there is something wrong? I mean, there sometimes is, but this time there isn't. Why jump to that conclusion?" He said that he'd been ill, and that was mostly it. "Okay, I guess I can see that. We're here to take you over to the gallery for some input. There are some of the pieces that we found that my father had stashed away that we're going to be putting out to sell. However, we haven't any idea how to price them. We're, mom and I, were hoping that you could help us with that."

"Why not ask the artist?" Andi looked at her mother before telling him that the man who had done the work had committed suicide a few weeks after her father had nearly destroyed him by not paying him the money due to him. They wanted to sell it to give to his widow and children. "So you want to sell it and give it to his estate, then. I like that idea. However, I'm not sure that I'd be the one to ask. You might want to talk to someone that has more experience in that sort of thing. I can recommend a couple of people that are trustworthy. But as for pricing it, that wouldn't be anything I'd be comfortable doing."

"Great." He gave them the names of the two people he'd met over the years. "We'll call them as soon as we get the gallery underway."

He was exhausted by the time he finished looking over the gallery. True to their word, they did a complete overhaul of the entire place. It was more open, and the walls that were up were only there to divide the room into sections that flowed nicely. Even the panels that divided up the areas were going to be used for more art. Loman was thrilled with what they'd accomplished in so little time. He couldn't wait for them to open so that he could come and see what his art looked like in the setting.

Loman was also very nervous about the showing. It would be his first one. He took pictures to sell to magazines, not to show off in this sort of setting. When Lindsley joined them after a meeting, he kissed her on the mouth and told her he loved what had been done.

"To be honest with you, this was more Andi and any of us." Andi immediately said that it was a team effort. That was something that he loved about his new family, how they were quick to give credit where it was deserved. "She decided that whatever father had had here, we'd do the opposite. The white walls and panels had been taken out by father some years ago. Since I'd not been spending as much time here, I didn't notice it until it was done. He'd had the walls in bright prints that would clash badly with the art. And he would have sculptures put on the floor. Like that would show them off in any kind of a good way."

They talked about what else they were planning as they made their way to the office. Lunch had been brought in for them, and he was glad for it. While in the darkroom, he'd forgotten to eat. It was like that all the time for him. He'd get involved in things and forget to fill his belly.

"How do you get your photos? I mean, I've seen some of your work. It's amazing. My favorite is the ones of the elephants. You must have been at the right place at the right time for those." He said he'd been there waiting for something to show up for hours. "Really? I had, well, I guess I figured you might have to wait for the next shot but not for hours."

"The last shot that I took was of some giraffes. A tower of them—it's what a group of them is called. They were having a treat of a tree that had only just come into some leaves. Also, there was a newborn calf with them." He didn't know if he should tell him the entire shot, so he told them about how he'd set up. "As it's been pointed out to me recently, I don't take a shower for days beforehand. I don't want to have them smelling me when I'm lying in waiting for them. So when they showed up, I had been there for about three hours. I was actually waiting on a group of zebra to come and enjoy some lunch. But they moved on before I could get them to come any closer. When the giraffes wandered over, they're magnificent creatures that I love to watch. It was the perfect opportunity to get a good shot of them."

"Anything ever come after you while you're waiting?" He told Andi he was a lion. "Oh, I guess you'd only have to shift, and they'd run away. I never thought of that."

"I won't shift unless I have to. Like I'm in danger or something. Mostly I just let a little of myself go, and that way, they can smell that I'm something bigger than they want to tangle with. If I were to shift, then smell like a lion, even shifting back, and nothing would come near me."

They talked about anything and everything while they sat there. Loman enjoyed himself immensely, and once they were headed home, he held Lindsley's hand as she drove them back to the house. It was a good day for him, and he was excited to start the next chapter of his life with his family.

~*~

When he came downstairs, Ronan was surprised to find Billy, Quinlan's daughter, in his kitchen. He loved the young girl and was happy for the help she gave everyone with her gift. She could talk to all animals and understood when they spoke back to her.

"Uncle Ronan, I need you to help me with something important. It's about a lion in captivity at a zoo." He asked her if she had eaten, and he smiled at her when she told him this was important. "He's dying, and he asked me for something. I don't have time to eat."

"You will eat, and then we'll talk. I've not had my breakfast, and I think better on a full stomach. Now, you can have a meal with me, go over what you know calmly, or you can come back when I've had my meal. All right?" She didn't look like she was going to sit down, but in the end, she did. "All right. I'm going to have eggs and bacon. What would you like?"

After getting her to agree to eat, he was happy to see that she enjoyed the meal with him. Ronan didn't know if he could help the young girl, but he would give it his best if he could. After their plates were taken away, he knew a little more about the lion in question.

"What zoo is he in?" She told him that he was out in California. "I don't even want to know how you were contacted by him. I'm assuming that it wasn't just a simple case of him getting in touch with you."

"No. It took a while for him to get to me. But now I can talk to him directly. He's old, very old, and he's never been anything but a lion in captivity. His mom was killed when he was no more than a cub, and then a group of men sold him to a person who had him roaming his lands. When the authorities found out, they took him and put him on display." Ronan asked her what he wanted from him. "He knows who you are. And he's very humble about what he is requesting from you. He would like to die as a freed lion."

Ronan had an idea that he was not going to like what the lion or Billy wanted. For a sixteen year old, she had a better head on her shoulders than most adults he knew. So if she had come to him about this, she knew just what she needed him to do. Leaning back in his chair, he asked her what the plan was.

"He's a good lion. Never has he caused any trouble at the place he's been in. But he knows that his death is coming. His body is worn out. When he dies there, they'll bury his body in some place with all the other animals that have gone on before him. Give him a marker that states his name and how long he'd been there. But that's now what he wants." Billy looked at him, and he could see that she was passionate about what she wanted. "He knows that he will pass on. However, he wants to be laid to rest on his own terms. Like his ancestors before him. King, what they call him at the zoo, wishes to simply be left where he dies so that the earth and its glory, he said, can take it back into itself."

"Where would you like for him to be able to die, Billy?" She said on the land that is here. The ranch that Robby owns. "He might not die as soon as we bring him here. What do we do with a full grown lion that cannot shift into a human? He'll need care, won't he?"

"No. He doesn't want that. What he wants is to be able to roam the lands as a free lion. I don't think he even knows what that means, but he won't bother anyone while he's here. He'll steer clear of the horses and other fenced-in animals that are on the ranch." He asked her if she'd figured out how they were going to get him here. "No. I only know that I want this to happen for him."

Ronan wasn't sure even where to begin in getting something moving on this. He wanted this to happen for Billy simply because he loved the young girl. Calling in his family and getting everyone involved, Ronan was able to get not just a meeting with the zoo president but also the vet that was caring for the animals that were in the park with King. Thanks to Rouge, Quinlan's mate who had some connections with the FBI. They had a meeting in three days.

"This lion, what happens if he tells every lion he is in contact with that this can happen for them? I don't want to be mean or rude, but I don't want to have to figure out a plan each time a lion or another animal wants to come here to die, honey." Billy stared at him. "Billy, what's really going on with this lion. This is more than just him wanting to die here. Tell me, please."

"I promise you, Uncle Ronan, it's just what I said. He's dying, and his last wish is to roam free." He didn't say anything. It wasn't as if he didn't believe her, but he felt there was something more. She told him all she knew about his life, some of it as bad as he'd ever heard of about a captive creature. "Haven't you just wanted to take a walk and not be bothered by fences or people getting in your way? Go to a store maybe and spend your money without anyone saying that you can't because of some stupid rule that you didn't agree to. Perhaps you wanted to go to a ball game or something like that. People around you have made it so that you can't get there. That the walls, big walls they've put around you are for your own good, they tell you."

"You really want this to happen, don't you?" She told him she wanted this more than she wanted anything in her life. "All right. I'll do my best. I'm not sure that it will work, but with this meeting that we're having, perhaps we can at least get someone to listen to us."

"Thank you, Uncle Ronan. You've no idea how much I appreciate this." After she left him, he sat there in his chair for several minutes, thinking about what he was doing. Having a lion, one that wasn't a shifter nor anyone that he knew was going to be roaming the lands. So many things could go wrong with this. Ronan was also sure with all the things that he was thinking about, there were millions more he'd not even thought of yet.

"Christ, I hope that I don't regret this." When Brook came home, he was feeling like he'd made a mistake. Tell her all the things that could go wrong with this, including the lion eating one of the humans, and she smacked him upside the head. Then she did it a second time. "What was that for?"

"Let me ask you something, dumbass." Ronan hated when she called him names. It meant that she was going to make him feel bad for thinking about whatever he'd had on his mind at the time. "Are you not the king of lions? That you are even the big deal over lions that aren't shifters?" He nodded. She popped him again, making his head bounce forward enough that his chin touched his chest.

"I'm not sure where you're going with this, but do you think you could stop popping me on the back of my head? I would like to have a few brain cells left when I get older." She told him to pay attention. "I will. With every part left of my brain. Now, what has you upset with me that I need to fix."

"You can just tell him not to eat anyone." He wanted to laugh. Like that was something that…he could do that, he remembered. "Don't give him too many rules. That's the point, right? That he wants his freedom. I'm not sure how this will work with King, but I'm willing to give it my all so he can have what he wants. I suppose it's not so much what he wants but more what he needs. I can understand it too."

After she left him alone in his office again, he

thought about his own freedom. Ronan did have quite a bit of freedom, but he thought, not nearly as much as he wanted. Shifters, even humans, were restricted in how they lived and worked. He let his mind think about what King had had to endure.

He'd been in captivity since he'd been a small kitten. Growing up in a household where he was able to roam the house wasn't all that good either. Billy had told him that King had been beaten when the master was upset. His food had been hit or miss, and sometimes they'd only allow him to have small portions of food rather than enough for a growing lion.

"He'd been beaten badly when one of his master's children had been playing with him, and King had clipped him with his paw. It hadn't been his fault as he'd tried to keep the child off of him. Once he'd been nearly killed by the man, the police were involved because of the child, and he was taken away to a large market where someone from the zoo had purchased him." He asked her if they were good to him. "I suppose so. They fed him well. Made sure that he was healthy and in good form. It wouldn't draw many people in if he was skinny and sickly, do you think? He'd get a bath. That was something else that he talked to me about. How he wanted to be able to swim in a river. He'd never done that as a kitten."

And that was something that Ronan himself loved to do. To shift to his lion and swim the river that was just inside of their property line. It was something that he was sure that his ancestors did when lions. It was the most fun he'd had in a long time. Being a cop before meeting Brook, he didn't get a lot of free time to get out and be himself. Or at least his other self. Ronan got up from his desk and went to find Rogue.

"Do you think this will be something that we can make work?" She asked him if he was willing to make a donation to the zoo. "Yes. I guess I should say a reasonable one, but Billy, nor for that matter, none of the kids have asked me for anything before, and I want to be there for her. For the lion as well."

"The meeting has been moved to the morning. I was going to go find you and see if you could go with me tonight. Bring Brook. She will be able to make them see reason if you can't." He asked his sister-in-law if she meant Brook would make them do what they wanted. "I'm reasonably sure that you know the answer to that. She's a hard ass, and she'll make it happen when she's passionate about something. However, even if they don't ask, I think you and her should make a nice donation to the zoo for the preservation of the lions' den. Hell, Ronan, you should just tell them what your plan is, and perhaps they'll be on board with that too. I don't know, but you can read their minds and see what they think."

"You want this as well, don't you?" She told him that she did. Not that she understood being a lion, but she could understand being boxed in and limited in what you could do. "Yes, I've been thinking about that as well. Like what would I do if I were trapped like that after having the freedom I have now."

"All right then. We'll leave as soon as Brook is ready to go. I'm hoping it'll only be for one night, but who knows." Rogue grinned at him. "At least we won't have to travel with a lion in a commercial plane if we get him. Parker said that once you land here, she'd pop him to the ranch as soon as we're on the strip to take off. I'm fucking excited to do this. I'm worried too but more excited."

Ronan was as well. But he was terrified. So many

things could go wrong, and he knew it more than anyone.

Chapter 3

Loman was going to take pictures of the lion when he arrived on their land. Having all his equipment with him, he was excited to do this for the big lion but mostly for his family. Not that anyone but his family would see the pictures, but he wanted them to be around so they could tell their children's-children about what they did for an animal of their kind. He thought he was more excited about that than just about any other picture he'd taken to date.

"Hey." He looked up at his brother Quin as he made his way to him. The plane had landed an hour ago at the airport, and they were waiting on Parker, with the help of Don, to bring the cage with King in it to them. Apparently, he'd been a good traveler and hadn't gotten upset once on the ride here. "I've been trying to contact you for the last couple of days. I keep getting sidetracked, what with all the things going on at the hospital and at home. You're about as healthy as I've seen you. How would you feel about being able to shift?"

It was almost as if his brother had commanded him to shift. His cat took him at that moment like he'd been on a mark in a sprinters race, just waiting for the gun to sound so he could take off. Loman had only a moment to appreciate being painless. A split second to feel like a new man and lion.

As Loman continued to run, letting his lion have his head, he saw King coming at him as if they were going to be side by side. Slowing just enough to let the lion catch up with him, King took the lead, and they ran straight to the trees. His lion seemed just as excited as he was to get to run with the older lion.

Jumping over fallen trees was his favorite thing to do. King, just slightly ahead of him, would leap through the air and take the ground on one paw. Almost as if he'd been doing it for years rather than his first time in the wild, so to speak. He bounced off of trees to make sharp turns. Leaves scattered in the air as he ran through them. Small animals scrambled to get cover as they ran over their hiding places. Loman was enjoying watching the playtime in front of him so much that he nearly fell twice instead of paying attention.

Loman didn't have any idea how long they ran. He only knew that he was having the time of his life. And that he'd never take for granted his ability to shift and run like this again. Also, he was going to make sure that his other half had more time out in the open.

Speaking to his family off and on a few times was great, but he ran with King wherever he wanted to go. Twice the cat had to stop to rest. He winded quickly. Loman didn't know if it was his age, being nearly twenty-six years old, or he simply wasn't used to running so much that slowed him down a few times. Loman himself wasn't used to running either, as a matter of fact. He'd been laid up himself for the last month. But King was magnificent in his recovery.

The river that ran the length of the ranch was something that King seemed to enjoy more than exploring caves. They both swam in the water and rested on the shorelines before getting back in the water or taking off again. When it began to get dark, he led the cat to the caves again to show him where there was shelter for him.

"I'm afraid that he won't stay there." He asked Billy who had spoken to him why not. *"He's enjoying his freedom in any way that he can. King wants to be out in the open, with the stars shining down on him. He told me he wants to wake in the morning with dew or snow on his coat because he can. I think that sometime soon, he's going to try and chase down his dinner. That's only a few of the things that he wanted by coming here. Uncle Loman, he told me that he had the best time with you today. That he couldn't have had a better time without you there with him. King said that he thanks you for taking time out of your day to be with him."*

"Tell him that it was my pleasure. That I think I enjoyed it much more than he did. It was something that I will likely never be able to do again. Run with a wild animal such as himself." He moved out of the cave and watched King as he found himself a place to lie down in the open area. *"He's been beaten up quite a bit, hasn't he? Like*

someone had used a whip against him. But he's never let it get him down today. I almost feel sorry for him but for him being here. Never once did he try to harm me or any of the other animals that are around here."

"He promised that he wouldn't. As for being beat up, *I don't know. I know that he's been depressed for a long time before he was able to contact me, I was told. I love what I can do for animals, but I find it to be so incredibly sad as well."* He told her what she did was good for all kinds of reasons. *"I know that. I've been able to save a lot of heartache for the animals here on the ranch. And I feel like I've been able to save a few lives, too, while I was at it."*

"Yes, you have. And you've been able to bring families together too." She laughed with him. *"I'm headed home. I think King is in for the night. I don't know that I could do this every day, but if you find out he wants a partner to run with, let me know. I did really enjoy myself today. As I'm sure, any of the others would as well if I'm busy."* She told him that she would pass that along to him.

As he made his way home as his other self, Loman couldn't believe how much better he felt. He wasn't sore anymore, for sure, but his body felt fit, and his mind was clearer than it had been in some time, he thought. He found himself wanting to get back to work too. Even his lion seemed to be better. While he still had to figure out who had poisoned him, he was content to pretend like he'd only had a horrible case of the flu or something and go on.

Lindsley was waiting for him when he got in the house. She had sandwiches and drinks for him, and he sat with her at the kitchen table as she told him about her day. He hadn't realized it was so late until the big grandfather clock in the hall chimed that it was two in the morning.

"I'm sorry you stayed up so late." She told him it was fine, as she wanted to talk to him anyway. "I'm so glad that you did. I've missed you today. But it's been a good day for me. I hope I didn't ruin any plans you might have had for us. When Quin told me that I could shift, I didn't think of anything else but getting out there and letting my lion go. And getting to run with an actual lion? Well, I don't know that many shifters can say that about themselves. He ran like he'd been out in the savannah for years."

"I got some pictures. Just with my phone. The two of you racing to the tree line was more than I could have hoped for in a photo of you two." He looked over the pictures she had taken and told her how great they were. And they really were too. "Not as good as yours are, but I'm pleased with them."

"I'll print them. I wanted to get some too, but, well, you see how that went." She told him that he'd been beautiful. "Thank you, love. But to have to admit that I thought that King looked great too. He really did enjoy himself. And when I left him, Billy contacted me, telling me that he didn't want to miss a moment of being outdoors. That tomorrow he was going to find his dinner and run it down. I wouldn't do that, but I can understand him wanting to. It would be one more thing that he could count as being free."

Loman had been sleeping in one of the spare rooms since he'd been able to get around on his own. Once they were at the top of the stairs, he kissed her quickly and headed toward his room. Once he was in there, he decided he smelled bad and decided to take a shower.

Even the hot water flowing over his body seemed to make an impact on his body. Loman had been down for too long with this thing that had happened to him.

Being poisoned with iron, quite a bit of it, he'd been told, had really done a number on his body. He'd forgotten how to be human, it felt like to him. Scrubbing his body as he thought about his next job, he nearly screamed like a little girl when the door slid open, and Lindsley stepped into the shower with him.

"Can I scrub your back for you?" Nodding, he turned when she asked him to. His mind was sort of frozen up with his body in that moment. "I bought some really nice sponges when I was in Columbus the other day. I don't care for the loofa ones. They're too hard on my skin. I think I have really soft and silky skin. What do you think?"

He touched his fingers to the arm she offered him. It was silky. When the hair on her arm danced under his fingers, Loman looked at Lindsley. Christ, he thought, he was going to be in big trouble if she wasn't hitting on him right now.

Her face was beautiful, like a soft cloud. Loman loved the way her face was put together. It sounded stupid, he knew, but as a photographer, he looked for things like that when he saw something he liked.

With her face damp from the heat of the water,

the dewy particles enhanced the freckles over her nose. The tiny hairs on her cheeks captured more water droplets and ran down her cheeks like a waterfall on a warm deserted island. He loved the color of her eyes, the way they would darken when she was angry or frustrated. Even now, they were darker than he'd ever seen them. He would be able to add lust to that list. Her lips, full and pink, seemed to beg for someone to kiss them.

Touching his fingers to her mouth, he was amazed at their warmth. Leaning down to her slowly, he kissed not just her mouth but her cheeks and nose as well. When she wrapped her arms around him, he picked her up and pressed her against the wall of the shower.

"This isn't how I envisioned us making love the first time." She laughed and told him that making love anywhere was all she'd been thinking about. "Then tell me, love, what took you so long to come to me?"

"I needed you to be healthy so that when you come the first time, you wouldn't be taking a nap because I wore you out. Or I broke you somehow." He laughed. Kissing her again, he lifted his head when she leaned her head away from him. "Loman, if you don't take me right now, I'm going to have to do something about it on my own. It's all I can think about is having you inside of me."

Turning off the shower, he took her to the bedroom. Lying her on the bed, still wet, he stood over her and looked at the most beautiful woman he'd ever seen. When she reached for him, Loman couldn't have asked for a better way to make love to the woman he'd come to love. Joining her on the bed, he spread her legs wide to see her in all her glory.

"Make love to me, Loman. I want to be yours in all ways." He wanted this to last, but he was having trouble concentrating on anything but having her. When she touched her fingers to her breasts, making her nipples harden, he watched as she slid her hands down her body to her oozing pussy. "I'm going to come."

It was glorious to watch her come. Her body tightened up, and her screams echoed in his heart as she called out his name. Even as she came a second time, Loman moved so that he could capture all her juices, lapping up all that she offered him.

Sliding his fingers into her sheath, he made love to her with his mouth and fingers. She came so many times that he lost track. Taking her fingers to his mouth, he licked them clean as he moved over her body. Sliding into her, she screamed again, tightening around his cock so wonderfully that he wanted to stay there forever.

Making love to her was something that he'd been thinking about since he first met her. It was nothing compared to the real thing. She was wonderfully responsive. Her body was in tune with his own. As he pulled her closer to him, pressing her body harder into the bed, he knew that so long as he lived, he'd never feel the way he did at this moment about another living creature. He was in love with his mate.

"Come with me, Loman. Now." He fucked her harder, bringing them both to their climax at the same time. When she begged him for more, he could not have turned her down, even with a gun to his head.

Loman emptied himself in his mate twice before realizing that he felt fulfilled. When she dug her nails into his back, holding onto him as she screamed out another release, Loman cried out himself as he came again and again before his body simply shut down.

When he woke up, Loman reached for Lindsley. When she wrapped her body around his, he held her tightly and thought of all the things that he was going to do now that he had a mate. First and foremost, he needed to figure out a way to work less so that he could spend more time at home with her.

"I don't think so." He looked at Lindsley when she spoke. "You talk in your sleep. Or awake, I'm not sure. But you're not quitting your job to stay home with me. I'd never get anything done, and you know it."

"You're saying that you'd chase me around the house all the time?" She just glared at him. "All right. I guess I can see where having me at home, getting under your feet as my mom used to say about my dad, would be a distraction."

"Distraction? You'd drive me crazy. You're a person that needs to be taking pictures. Your mom told me about your first job. I can't imagine you at eight, much less taking pictures." He told her that it had come easy for him. "That right there is what I'm talking about. You not being able to get out and take pictures. And do not mention to me that you could take pictures of kids in a studio. That would make you insane, and you know it. No. You need the wild and outdoors more than anyone I've ever met."

When she got up to take a shower, he wasn't sure if she was mad at him or not. The more he thought of it, the more he wondered if he should be upset. Getting up, he took a shower too, making love to her again, he decided that neither of them was mad, but he'd better be finding himself a new job to do, or he'd be in dutch with the missus, as his dad used to say.

Loman decided to start writing those old sayings down. He'd feel closer to his father if he did that. He also knew the perfect person to help him. Grandda would get a kick out of it because he was sure that his dad got them from his dad.

~*~

Lindsley was cleaning out the desk that had been in storage since her father had taken over the gallery some years ago when her mom joined her. She'd had a meeting this morning and was still dressed in her suit. Lindsley asked her how it had gone.

"Well, I think. I'm glad that we never had a board here. My goodness, they're very tight-fisted with their money. Carmilla was there as well. When she invited me to be a part of the hospital board, I didn't have any idea that she was the president of it." Lindsley asked her why that would make a difference. "None, I suppose. I was—what are you doing there?"

"This desk was once grandpa's, and I wanted to use it in my office. But the drawers are stuck or locked. I can't get them open." Mom came to the other side of the desk where she was. "The top one will open, but the others won't. And I've searched everywhere for a key, but there doesn't seem to be one."

"Look under the desk." She said she couldn't lift the sucker. "Yes, I think that might have been my dad's plan. He used to hide things like credit card applications when they came in under the desk so that he could burn them in the fire later. It wasn't until he was able to get a shredder that he stopped doing that. I have an idea. Ask the men here to help you. Aren't you having some work done here with some of the Foster men? Perhaps they can lift it up for you."

After calling for a couple of them to come and help, Cass and Quin teased her when they found her on the floor with all sorts of kitchen tools in front of her. Quin asked her what she thought a pair of tongs was going to do to get the desk open.

"For your information, I was using the tongs to pull out paper. If I ever found any. Grandda was good at keeping things forever. And I wasn't positive that I wanted to touch something that might have been in here for decades. I just wanted to take this to my office and use it." Quin said that it was a great idea. "Thank you. Now, if you guys could just lift it up enough so I can look under it, I'd be happy."

The key was there. Stapled to the bottom of the desk in a way that she had to have the desk tipped over so that she could work to get it off. Just as soon as she had the key in her hand, they lifted the desk back up and set it on its bottom. However, it was Cass who noticed that some papers had been dislodged and asked her if she wanted to look at them.

"They appear to have come from a panel on the bottom." She agreed with her mom and picked up the papers that had been unearthed. While she was at that, Cass unlocked the drawers for her. "What are they, honey?"

"I'm not sure what I'm looking at. They look like

deeds to something. But it's worn where the state is. I don't think it's here. But it looks like grandda only paid about fifty-three cents an acre for whatever this is." Handing it to Cass when he asked, she pulled the rest of the papers to her that he'd been able to pull from the locked drawers. "Here are more deeds, mom. Did you know that grandda was buying up property?"

"It would have been before her time. Look at the dates of purchase." She could see that now. Whatever he bought, it was about ten years before he'd even met her grandmother. "I can have someone look into these for you. There would be records. And since it has the number of the book as well as the line number, it would only take someone a couple of minutes to pull the right deed book to look it up."

"Do you think that he still owns it?" Cass told her that it was hard to tell after so many years. "All right. You do that, and I'll see what else I can—" Lindsley looked at her mom. "This is a bank key, mom. Remember Grandda telling us that he'd lost one? I think…Andi might remember if he told us which bank it was from."

When Parker just popped into the room, it nearly

scared ten years off her life. Asking for the key, she handed it back almost immediately. The look on her face wasn't quite a smile, but it wasn't evil-looking either. Mom asked her what she had found out.

"This is the key that your father was looking for. He didn't want your husband to find it accidentally and go to the bank. Your dad was a smart man, Meggie, if you didn't already know that." She said that she had, but Allen hadn't been running the gallery by the time her dad had died. "No. But he must have figured he would at some point. You should go to the bank and open the drawer. It's a large one, so if I were you, I'd take my daughters with me."

Since it was still early afternoon, she abandoned the desk in favor of going to the bank with her mom. Andi was going to meet them there as she'd had an appointment with another artist that might well be a part of their grand opening. While they were gone, the desk would be moved to her office and cleaned up. She wanted to be there when it was set, but Cass promised her that he'd help her move it if it wasn't in the right place.

As soon as her mom asked the banker if she could

open the box, he had to go and look it up. When he came out of his office, he looked so strangely at them that Lindsley just knew that it wasn't going to pan out to be anything. Disappointed, she was shocked when he told her the box numbers. Not one box but a few of them

"As far as I know, no one has opened the boxes since it was purchased sixty-seven years ago. At some point, your father came in and added your name, Ms. Benson as another person that could get into the box along with your mom. Your signature is there on that line." Mom laughed and said she remembered doing this. She'd been about eight years old. Then she asked about how it wasn't a rental but a box her dad had purchased. "When the bank first opened, there wasn't a big demand for renting boxes to store things in. I don't think people were willing to trust banks yet, so they sold them in order to pay for some of the costs of having them put in. I think your father was the first one to buy them. The number on his drawers are one through seven."

"Wait, there are seven drawers that belonged to Grandda?" Mr. Elfish told her he'd been there when they were bought but never thought of them again since before his passing. "Elfish. You…?"

"Yes, my dear. I'm an elf, or better yet, a fae." She hugged him, and he laughed. "Well, that was very welcome but unexpected. How about we get you ladies into the vault and see what it is that your relative saved for you."

Mom was going to open the first drawer. But before she could insert the key into the lock, she handed it over to her. Telling her that since she'd found the key that she should have the honors. Putting the key into the lock, she was surprised at how easily it slid in and opened. Pulling the drawer out, she sat it on the table before pulling open the lid. It was one of the larger drawers in the vault.

"Wait." They both turned to Andi. "Let's get three of them out so that we can each look into the boxes all at the same time. I don't know if that's a good idea or not, but I want to have the element of surprise myself. This is so exciting that I'm about to pee myself."

"Andi. What a thing to say." They all three laughed. Once Lindsley was able to pull the two drawers from the wall, she sat them on the table with her box. "Well, what do you say, my dears? On the count of three?"

Pulling open the lid when mom said three, Lindsley was slightly disappointed in her box. Then as she began pulling out the ugly leather bags and feeling their weight, she opened the first one and poured it out into her hand. Uncut diamonds.

There were perhaps two dozen of them laying in the palm of her hand when Andi put her hand next to hers. Hers were uncut rubies. Mom had emeralds. They stared at the gems without saying a word. That was when Jasper and his mom joined them.

"They're yours, aren't they?" Andonna shook her head and smiled. "Then they're yours, Jasper. Right? There is no way that my grandda had all these locked in a safety deposit box for all these years and it being legal."

"Oh, they're yours now. Had you not opened this, I would never have put the man I once knew to your grandda, Lindsley. He was a very, very good friend of mine." Mom asked her how he'd come to have them. "He found them in the other realm when looking for a flower for me. As it turned out, he found a great many plants that I thought were all gone for me. This, these gems that he found seemed little payment for what he gave me in return."

"A flower?" Jasper explained that the flower he'd been looking for had been used almost to extinction. When his mom had hired her grandda to find the bushes that the flower grew on, because it seemed that he had a knack for finding lost things, he would dig up the plant and find gems of all sorts in the roots of them. "I'm sorry. So you let him keep what he found? That's a great deal of money even if there was only one of them."

"This is going to sound simply terrible, but in our realm, where we live most of the time, we have no use for money. Gems yes. They decorate the walls and crowns. All sorts of things like that. But not for any kind of monetary gain." Putting the diamonds back in the bag, she emptied a second one the same way. "Those are moonstones. Very valuable in this world. Anyway, once your grandda found the first bush, its root system was damaged by all the gems. It was what was making them hard to grow. Once he was able to locate a dozen of the bushes, he figured out a way for us to grow them without harming them. Not only that, but he also showed us how to break the roots into smaller bushes so that we could propagate them easily in the gardens he helped us put together."

"So this is all from a dozen plants?" It was Andonna who explained this time. "I guess I can see where that would be helpful. Knowing how to find them after grandda showed you would have given you a larger crop to work with. But I don't understand why you gave him all this. Couldn't you have, I don't know, invested it into something else?"

"We did in your grandfather. After he was successful in finding the flowers that we needed, it was a simple thing for us to hand over a list of things that we thought too were nevermore. But he was not only able to find nearly everything on the list, but he was also able to make it so that we knew how to dry the seeds as well as work with the roots. Your grandda was a brilliant man." Mom said that he'd never said a word about it. "No, he'd not. He told us once that he was going to make it so that his children, if he ever had any, would not have to work as hard as he did to make a living. The gallery at that time was closed down due to men going off to war."

They went through each of the bags. There were ten in the first drawer and a dozen or more in the next five. Each of them had gems in them, all uncut but for the last drawer. There were tiny bags in the drawer, filling it from top to bottom of seeds.

Each of them was marked with what they were. There was paperwork in the bottom of it, written in her grandda's handwriting on how and when to seed them. Not only that but things they could be used for such as illnesses and wounds.

Jasper and his mom were more excited about them than they were about the gems. When asked if she wanted to take them back to her castle, she declined, saying that someday there might be a need for such seeds and it would be nice to know that they were safely hidden away to be used.

"Would they still be viable, you think?" Andonna only had to put her hand on one of the bags to know they were just as viable as they had been when he'd sorted them out and put them away. Mom held one bag of the seeds to her chest, sobbing. "He was a better man than I could ever have imagined, my dad. Oh, how I wish he was here so that I could tell him again how much I loved him."

The three of them hugged. She missed him as well. And her dad. They'd been taken from them much too early. Oh, to have them both around to meet Loman and his family. When they were ready to go, they had to decide what to do with the drawers of gems. It was Andi that had a good idea.

"Leave them here. We know they're in the bank, so we don't have to worry about it right now. I guess someone could come in and try to get to them, but so long as no one knows they're here, we should be all right until we think of something." Andonna said that since Mr. Elfish was here, no one would ever find the gems. Mom thought that was a great idea. "Good. I hope you like this one as well. I think we should each take one gem from each bag to have something made in a way that would remind us of our grandda and dad, not all at once. That would—" Jasper laughed before speaking.

"I'd gladly do that for you. That way, no one would have to know that you have them, and I can fashion a lovely necklace or bracelet—anything you like really and a jeweler wouldn't know a thing about it." She and Andi agreed it should be mom first since it was her dad. "Excellent idea. Yes, I love that. Once you figure out what you want in the way of a piece, I'll do that for you. Anytime you wish."

After leaving all the gems at the bank, they decided to go to dinner, just the three of them. They'd been working so hard on the gallery that they felt they deserved a night off together. Careful about what they spoke about, not bringing up the gems at all, they had a good time relishing in the fact that their dad hadn't found the key before they had.

Chapter 4

Loman had hated to leave home this time. He thought it was the first time in all his adult life that he felt that way. He had a family now, and they were the most important thing to him. Just as he was about to get up and get his butt home, he saw the American bison coming over the crest of the hill. Christ, they were a lot of them.

"I have a question for you." He told Parker he was slightly busy but could answer a simple question for her. *"Good. I was wondering if you've given any thought to having a studio for your work? I don't mean a gallery. You have access to one. I was thinking more along the lines of a*

place where you could develop your pictures and do whatever it is you do to them to make them beautiful."

"First of all, they're beautiful when I take them." They both laughed as he took several shots of the herd moving in his direction. *"I have a dark room set up at the house. I guess it's not really large enough for what I wanted, but I have — why? Do you have an idea where I can have a place all to myself?"*

"I do. Remember me telling you about the daycare center that went belly up a few months ago? Because the basket company no longer employing hundreds of people with children, they couldn't make a go of it. Anyway, it's coming on the market in the next few days. While we do have the need for a daycare center, it would be cheaper to tear that one down and start over. But you could use it for your work." He asked her where it was located. *"You see, that's the issue I'm having with it too. It's smack dab in the middle of town. I mean, right across the street from the courthouse. Brook was telling me that when it was finished being built, it was already out of date. But they had a need for it, and they sort of looked the other way when it came to codes. It would need to have a few walls taken down. Bathrooms updated. Unless you like having toilets about three inches from the*

floor. Also, the office needs to be enlarged. If you have a need for one. Brook also suggested that you put in a loading dock. The building is big enough right now that you could actually divide it in half and rent out the other side."

"*I'd rather not."* Parker said that she thought he'd say that. "*All right. I'll give this some thought. If there isn't anything else pressing, I have a herd of very large American bison coming at me, and I'd like to not get crushed."*

"*They won't touch you if you want to stay where you are."* He asked her if she'd done something to keep him safe. "*Forever, Loman. Just stay there, and you'll get the shots that you want. I'll talk to you later."*

True to her word, he was never stepped on. Not even close. However, he was able to get some of the best shots of a herd that he'd ever been able to get before. Close-ups of them eating the spring grass as it sprouted. Mothers nursing their young being watched over by the herd. He was even able to capture a goodly amount of pictures of a pack of wolves moving along with them, keeping pace.

After they passed over him, Loman got up, collected his equipment and moved to the top of the ridge where the herd had come from. He'd been meaning to make his way there for the last few days, but now that he'd gotten so many shots down below, he felt better about heading to the spring lake that had appeared overnight during the rainstorm.

Making his way there slowly, he could see that there was a mother bear and her two cubs. Even as a lion, Loman was terrified of grizzly bears. They were meaner than the black bears he'd heard. But once again, Parker reminded him that he'd be safe.

As the afternoon turned into evening, Loman was surprised at the different animals that came to graze at the water hole. He knew it was a popular place to view some of the animals. A tour drive in the summer months would drive by this area in hopes of seeing some of the animals.

Bighorn sheep and elk in smaller groups wandered by but didn't come to the waterhole to drink. With his camera, he was able to get some good pictures of them, even with the distance they were from him. Loman had been able to get a good shot of a moose and her calf. Christ, it was as if they'd been just waiting for him to come around to get some candid pictures of them today. Something occurred to him, and he reached out to Parker.

"*No. I had nothing to do with you being able to see all of the animals at once. However, you might want to ask Jasper about it. When you were down this time, he gave you a bit more of himself. Being fae, or at least having a bit of it in your bloodline, could be what is attracting them to you.*" He asked how much he'd given him. "*I don't know. But I know he had to rest for several days before he could come and check on you. Also, he was able to find the person that poisoned you.*"

He paused in his work to think about what she said. "*Was it a man by the name of Winston Greene?*" She asked him how he'd known. "*He sent me a nice parting gift a few weeks ago. He wanted to be my agent — he was actually kind of aggressive about it. But in the end — anyway, it was tea, the loose-leaf kind. While I'm not a big fan of hot tea normally, I had the first cup and enjoyed it very much. After it was all gone, it was like I no longer had an addictive drug to take. It took me a month to get to the point where I didn't crave it.*"

"*I'll take care of him.*" He wasn't sure what that meant and decided he didn't want to know what she did. "*Loman, you can ask me. I'll tell you what my plans are for him. I don't think you'll like it. However, I will tell you that you're not the first nor the last person that he's done this to. His plan is, now that I have seen his mind was to poison you enough where you'd come to him for more tea. You'd be, he hoped, desperate enough to give him what he wanted to get more of the drugs that he put in the tea. Greene has killed a lot of people with this method."*

"Then you have at him. But I'd like for you to make him understand that he's not just someone you're out to take care of randomly. He needs to know the reason that you're there." She said that he would, she promised. *"Thank you. If you need it, I have the tin that he gave the tea in with me. I haven't any idea why I kept it. I suppose to remind me not to be so easy next time someone gives me a gift."*

When he was finished, the darkness making it so that the larger predators came out, he made his way back to his hut. It was nothing more than a tent that was covered in brush, but it was warmer than sleeping out in the open. As soon as the sun went down in the mountains where he was, the temperature would drop as much as thirty degrees at night. Just as he was pulling his sleeping bag up and over his body, he felt the death of King.

"He's gone." He told Billy that he'd felt it too. *"He's gone, Uncle Loman. He told me that he loved what we'd done for him and that he was at peace. What am I going to do now?"*

"Nothing, honey." Loman rubbed his heart, the pain there for the death of someone that he only just realized was a friend. *"You made it so that he got a last wish. King got to die on his own terms, and that is the best thing that any of us could hope for. I'm so very sorry for your loss, but honey, you did such a wonderful thing in what you did for him. And for me. You fulfilled something in me that I would never have gotten without your gift. Thank you for that."*

"I'm to let him lay where he died. I feel so horrible about promising him that. The animals will – they'll get to him." He told her that was the way that he wanted it. *"I can't stand it. I wish that I'd not promised him that."*

"You'll do that for him, correct? You'll let him stay where he died?" She said that she'd promised. *"Good for you. In a few months, we'll put a marker there that tells all who pass by that a great lion had died there. It will be fitting for him."*

"I love that idea." He was glad. *"Thank you so much*

for being there for me. You've been a good friend to him and to me. Even though we're not really related, I think of all the Fosters as my true family."

She couldn't have said anything else to make him happier than he was at this moment. Wiping away the tears as he settled into his bed, he thought of all the things that he wanted to do now. Lindsley had been right. He needed the outdoors like he needed his next breath.

Stopping by the office on his way out, he told the Park Rangers that he'd seen a couple of newborn bison that were struggling. They'd go and check it out, but they'd not interfere. It was the way that it worked in the big park.

It took him less time to get home than it had to get to the park. Yellowstone was a beautiful place to go and get the kind of pictures that he wanted and that his clients wanted. Since he had about five hours to kill before he met with one of the people that wanted some of his work, he decided to go and have dinner at one of his favorite places to eat. He was thrilled beyond words when not only Parker and Don joined him but also Ronan and Brook.

"I've been meaning to ask you, how do you keep anonymity when you go and talk to clients that want to feature your work in their magazines? I mean, you've so far kept the world from knowing who you are. I'm just curious how that works." He told Ronan that they thought they were talking to his representative. Ronan laughed long and hard about that. "They have no idea that the very artist is the one they're working with? Oh, Loman, I knew you were good before this, but you're better than I thought. I'm betting you can keep your work the way you want it too."

"I do. This guy I'm seeing this afternoon is a first-time buyer. I've sent him the price ranges for how many pictures he might want. But so far, all I've heard back from him is that he wants all I took." Brook asked if he'd sell them all to him. "Yes, for a price. These are the picture that I took about three months ago. I have a contact sheet that he can look at. Also, they're on a thumb drive as well. He can look at them either way."

"Aren't you worried about him just printing them and using them without paying? That would be something I'd be worried about." He told him what he'd been able to do. "So if he tries to print them in any way but the contact sheet that is on the thumb drive, or even if he tries to enlarge them, it'll lock up his computer? That's good but aren't you worried about him suing you for that? I mean, shutting down a computer seems like that would be a good way to get your ass handed to you."

"He has to sign off on the rules and regulations before he can have the drive. Once he does that, he can look at the photos at his leisure for thirty days. After that, the drive will be blank." He looked over at Parker when she smiled. "I don't know what I'd do without having a bit of magic in the family. I thank Parker every time someone calls me and says that their computer is no longer working or, better yet, they can't print off the photos."

"You think this guy is going to try and do that, don't you?" Loman nodded at Don. "Want me to go with you? I can do a little extra to his computers if you want. It would be my pleasure."

"I'd love for you to go, but you don't have to. I think this guy is going to try and shaft me in some way. Much like Allen did. Getting something for nothing." Don nodded and said he'd go. "Thank you.

I'd appreciate that. By the way, what brings you guys here? I'm sure that it's more than having lunch with me."

"I'm here to take care of some Pride business. There is a pride close to here that wishes to move to California. They want to go where the jobs are, and they think that it will be a good move for them. I'm not so sure, but I'm going to allow it. There are eight brothers and two sisters. The sisters are married with cubs of their own. Once they're able to get things set up on the other end, they'll follow with their parents. Two of the men, I don't remember their names right now, but they're going to be—Tucker. That's their name. Those two will stay here to help the pride they're leaving be prepared for their exit. I don't know that the pride that they're leaving will survive after they lose a dozen of the members. But that's something the pride leader will have to deal with on his own. They wish to be known as the Tucker Pride." Brook said that they're setting up their own group. A family affair much like the one they have. "I'm sort of glad that they're going out there. I have a few small prides out there but nothing that is doing all that well. I'm excited for them to get a start fresh. I just hope that they can. It will be nice for all of them."

After they were finished with their lunch, he and Don made their way over to the office of the Short Becker Magazine office. Don made fun of the name, and they were still laughing about it when they were told they could have a seat and that Mr. Becker would be with them soon as he was running behind.

"I have an appointment for four o'clock. I want to return home as soon as this meeting is over to talk to *my* client. Could you tell him that I don't have all day?" She said that he'd be with them as soon as he could. He was running behind. "So you said. Twice now. If we're not in his office by four, we're leaving. My client, as you are aware, is a busy person. I won't wait around if I don't need to."

"Hard ass, are you?" He told Don that he was like that with all his appointments. *"Another side of you that I'm surprised by. Good job. But will you really leave at four if you're not where you're supposed to be?"*

"I have before." When it was two minutes until four, the secretary looked at them. She didn't say anything as she answered her phone, but she looked very uncomfortable. *"I have a feeling she doesn't like this any more than I do."*

At one minute after four, they stood up and left without a word. He was in the lobby when the security guard told them that Mr. Becker could see them now if they were to return to the office. Loman handed him his badge that he and Don needed to get into the building and left. It was a refreshing feeling to be in charge of his life.

~*~

Denver stood up when the king entered the room. He had to fight hard not to lie on the floor and submit to him. But it was a public setting, and humans wouldn't understand the way that someone treated a man like the new king was.

"Mr. Foster, I'm very glad that you were able to come and speak to me." He sat down when asked. But he couldn't until his king and Queen did. Once they were both seated, he did the same. "My family is working with our pride leader and are making sure that we're not going to devastate him too terribly bad when we leave."

"I've spoken to him. He told me that there isn't

a better family around than your family. He also said that if anyone could make it out there, it would but the Tuckers. Why don't you tell me what you're plans are once you're out on your own." Denver pulled out his notes. He was forever keeping up with himself but making notes. "Good. If you don't have something to make notes on or to read from, you'll fail. My wife taught me that."

"Good for you, my ladyship. My mom. She's a great note-taker. She usually has about five lists going at any given time. All of them are labeled as to what they're for and a timeline on when she wants to get them finished." He smiled at the memory of his first notebook. "When we were headed to school, she handed each of us a nice notebook to take with us. You've no idea how many times it saved me from being late on an assignment, your lordship."

"You're a potter. I've seen your work. It's lovely. I have a brother that is an artist as well." He told his queen that two of his brothers were artists in different fields. He called her his ladyship again. "If you call me my queen once more, I'm going to bash your head in. I'm Brook. This is Ronan. If we're going to make this work, we have to be on the same page. If I have to keep looking around for who you're talking to, it's not going to work."

He wasn't entirely sure if she was really going to hit him but didn't call her anything more. When asked if he'd start on his list, Denver was very careful of what he said. The more time he spent with the couple, the more he thought she really would hurt him.

By the time he got his list taken care of, he was on the road to making a more extensive list. Not only did they both have suggestions on how they could make things work, but they also offered them some of the Pride money to get them started. His family was worried about housing, and Brook told him that they owned a house there and would let them use it so long as they were careful of the upkeep.

"I have contacts all over the world, Denver. If you need anything at all once you're out there, you just pick up the phone." Denver thanked them both. "If you're struggling and don't ask for help, then we can't help you. We can't fix what we don't know about. All right?"

"My parents are mostly worried about what sort

of jobs we can get while out there. I know that being an artist isn't really a huge income sort of job for us right now, but we're going to find jobs that can sustain our family first and foremost." Brook asked what the others did. "Mostly manual labor. That's why we wanted to do this. One of my brothers has a law degree, and two of them are doctors. They all work in their field, but it doesn't really pay all that much because they're fresh out of college. Taking on jobs that put food on the table is the only thing we're doing right now."

After making a few phone calls, not only did his brothers have a job, but his parents—really, his grandparents had help in the home as well. Denver was shocked by the amount of help they were getting from the king and queen. He was still making notes when Ronan asked him if he had plans for his sisters' children.

"You mean in ways of getting them into a good school? If so, then yes. Margo, my older sister, is a teacher. She was actually a headmistress at one of the schools around here until it closed down. Lack of funding. She has been applying online to teach at a couple of private schools." Again they were helpful in getting Margo a good job in one of the private schools that she'd not applied for because you needed references that she didn't think she had. "I don't know how to thank you for this. I think that everyone in my family will be grateful to you both for decades to come. This is much more than I could have hoped for when – I actually expected you to tell me that it wasn't going to work and that we had to stay where we were."

"I'd never do that. Even if you were taking the entire pride apart with this move, I'd want you to succeed. There is a need for people like your family. Branching out is difficult enough without having support and funds to make it work." Brook told him how she'd torn her house apart nearly daily to learn how to do some of the jobs that are on a construction site. "So you see, we know what it's like to want something bad enough to take a chance that you might normally never do. I hope your parents are very proud of all of you."

"They are. Well, grannie is. Grandda, he's a little…grumpy about having to move. He'll do what grannie tells him, but he won't show anyone he's happy about it. Then once it's all setup and working, he'll take some of the credit." Denver laughed. "He's a wonderful man, and I've loved him with all my heart since they took us all in when our parents left us. He'll do what is necessary, but he doesn't have to be quiet about how much we're putting him out to do it."

"I have my grandda too. And my mom. My father passed away some time ago, and I miss him so much. But having my mom and grandda, I know what you mean about them being grumpy. My grandda can be that way as well." Brook didn't add anything to the conversation this time, and he decided that was all right too. He really liked the two of them and hoped that someday he'd be able to invite them to his home and show them what all their help had done for them. "You have your family make a list of things that they're going to need to travel, and we'll make the arrangements for you all when it's time. Just don't forget to call when you need something, Denver. All right?"

Shaking hands with the two of them, he felt something akin to an electrical shock move up his arm and over him. It was stronger from the king, but it was no less painful from the queen herself. Once they were finished with all the notes that they both had brought to the table, he was invited to have dinner with them. Once the food was ordered, two of Ronan's brothers showed up, and he got another shock from them. Christ, he wondered what it meant but didn't mention it to anyone there.

On his way home, he reached out to his family. He had to calm himself several times before he was able to speak about the things that were said. Grannie was the most excited about her and Grandda having help in their home. But his sisters were happy that they were going to be able to start working almost as soon as they arrived.

After he got home, he talked to his grandparents. When Grannie heard that the queen's name was Brook and that she owned a construction company, she paled a little. After asking if she was all right several times, she told him what she knew about Brook Garret and her family. He'd not had a clue.

"That's why she didn't mention her own family when I was talking to them about you guys. I did wonder about that. Even if the newspaper told only half of what she had to endure, I wouldn't have been able to do it. And she made something of herself too." He also understood a little more as to why they wanted to help people when they were starting out. The Fosters, now that he knew about the others in the family, were about the richest people around. Not to mention a lion pride. His respect for the king and queen went up a great deal. He was excited about this next phase of his life working with someone so generous as they were.

"She mentioned paying it forward once we're set up. I really like that idea. I don't know that we'll be able to do it on the scale they do, but hiring people that need a hand-up is something I can get behind. I'm to understand that she mostly hires ex-cons to get them trained to be able to work for something else. And she pays all her people a fair wage too." His brothers, like him, were taking notes on the information he was sharing. "They're going to set us up when we start this move. I'll do whatever they want to make this work for all of us."

And he would too. Denver and his family had been talking about this move for a while now, and they were ready to go. But having support was going to make it much easier than he thought when he first approached Ronan and Brook.

Chapter 5

Loman didn't move. Not that he could stop himself from blinking, but he was nearly too afraid—not afraid but freaked out to do more than stare at the…whatever it was across from him. It seemed to be comfortable to be just sitting on the shelf and swinging its little legs. Loman was trying his best not to run out of the room screaming.

It was about a foot tall. It had wings, so he knew it had to be something magical. Actually, he didn't know that for sure until it pulled a feather duster from the air and wiped down the books it was leaning against. It even tisked at him. Like it was disappointed in him for having a dusty shelf.

The ears on it were high and pointed but not really out of proportion to its body. There were piercings on both of them too. Or maybe it had been born with the shiny objects in its ears. Its body was blue. Which, to him, was a lame way to say what color it was. He thought of ocean waters at the deepest point he'd seen on some of his expeditions. Or a sky when a small cloud burst was about to happen where you could actually see it coming toward you from a distance. She tisked at him again.

"I'm not an 'it' but a female." He nodded, not sure if it had spoken or not. "If you think of me as an 'it' once more, I'm going to smack you. And it'll hurt too. I'm a female. Fae. I was sent here by Lord Jasper and his queen mother. Several days ago."

"Why?" He giggled a little when the female tisked at him again. "Look, I'm trying very hard to believe that you're here and that you're real. I was only sitting here, minding my own business, when I sighted you out of the corner of my eye. And you're tisking at me. I don't know that I care for a creature around that is going to take me to task about a little dust."

"'Tis more than a little dust, and someone should have been cleaning it up before now." He asked her if that was her job. "Nay. I'm not a dust bunny to clean up after the likes of you. I'm a companion." He wasn't entirely sure what a companion might be to her way of thinking, but he nodded at her. "Look here, Lord Loman, I was told to find you and make myself known to you several days ago. But you were gone. I've been here, sitting on my bottom, waiting for some word that you were to return. Now that you have, I'm testy."

"Testy? I'd say you're a bit more than just testy. You're very rude. So, now that we've established why you're here and your job description is—well, I guess some of it, perhaps it's time that you tell me your name." She told him that he'd have to give her one. "No. I won't do that. If you've had no name before coming here, then you'll have to give yourself one. If you've had one before today or whenever you were about, then that's what I'll call you."

"I was called Amerdan when I was brought to the castle to serve the queen." He said that he liked that name if she did. "What do I care what my name is when you call me. So long as you continue to call me—"

He whistled to shut her up. "You will have to take your rudeness down a few notches when we're speaking. If you have no desire to be here working with me or for me, then I'd rather you went back to where you came from. I've no time for someone nipping at me every time you open your mouth. Now. Do you want to be here or not?" She said that she was here, wasn't she? "Yes, you are. But that isn't anything near what I asked you. Do you want to be here, or should I send you home? I don't want to have to sort through your anger all the time to figure out what it is you need to tell me or ask me. It's very taxing on a person to have a pissed-off person around them. Either we get along, or you go home. That's final."

"I've only been this angry since I arrived three days ago. I don't know why. Do you?" He didn't have an answer for her and said as much. Then asked her if it was because she had to wait on him. "Perhaps. It would have been nice if you had told me that you weren't going to be here when I arrived."

"Since I had no idea that you were going to be here at all, I couldn't have done that, now could I?"

She told him that the queen was to tell him that she was coming. "No one told me anything. When you — I haven't any idea how you came to be here, but seeing you was the first time that I knew of you. I'm still in the dark a bit about why you're paired up with me. Or why anyone would think that I'd need a companion. I have a very large family, and now my wife and her mother and sister. That's usually more than enough for a person to be around. So, again, I ask you, why are you here?"

"I'm to be a companion to you, is what I was told. Your mate, she'll have a fae too. His name is Mitar." He asked her to define what she thought she could do for him as a companion. "I can go and get things for you that you might need. I have noticed that you take a great many pictures. I can help you with that by having things ready for you should you need them. If you are hungry for a certain food, I can get that for you as well. I will do things for you that will save you time and energy. I'm magically enhanced so that I can see to your every need."

"All right. That clears things up a little. While here, where will you stay? I'm assuming that you'll be around all the time." She said that she only needed an hour a day to rest on him. "I'm sorry? Rest on me?"

She flew at him and up the sleeve of his shirt. As she moved around under his sleeve, he could feel the pinch of her hands as she used her fingers to climb up his arm. As if she were searching for a place to tear off his skin. Then, just as suddenly as she stopped moving, he could feel her under his skin.

Pulling off his shirt, he could see that a smaller version of her was on his arm just above his elbow. But it was her wrapped around his arm, like a tattoo, that freaked him out again. He tried to pull her off, digging into where her body was at his muscle, but there was no budging her. When she moved, crawling up his arm to his shoulder and to his back, he stood very still while she aligned herself with his spine. Christ, he could feel her breathing. Her heart beating with his. Loman looked up when Lindsley came into the room with her T-shirt off and a male version of what he had on his back on her arm.

"It's on me." He cautioned her about calling it an it. "That's all you can say to me right now? That not to call whatever this is an 'it'? What the hell is going on?"

"Don't freak out more than I am right now. One of us needs to be calm, or I'm going to lose my shit. So today, you're the calm one. Okay? How about you sit down with me and—wait, take a picture of her. Her name is Amerdan. Your fae is Mitar. Anyway, take a picture of her so that I can figure out why I can feel her wrapped around my spine. Please?" She did what he asked. While she was busy taking the picture for him, Mitar moved up and over Lindsley's shoulder to her back and did the same as Amerdan had done. Wrapped around her spine. "I have a feeling that this is something that we're going to have to get used to."

"I don't think so. This creature...Mitar, he just appeared while I was in the kitchen and slammed his body into my arm. I could feel it moving over me, Loman. Under my fucking skin." He nodded. "You'd better have more to say to me right now than the rattling of your fucking head. I'm fucking freaked out here."

"Andonna was supposed to let us know they were coming. I'm not sure what happened there, but I saw Amerdan there on the shelf, and she was pissed off because I wasn't here when she arrived. She's somewhat of a bitch." Now she nodded at him. "I'm assuming that Mitar was as well?"

"He didn't speak but just became a part of me. I don't know that I like this, Loman. Why are they here?" He told her what Amerdan had told him. "Companion? All right. I guess...no, I don't understand. Andonna come here now, please?"

Surprising the shit out of him, the queen appeared in the room. She was holding a cup in her hand and as well as a few cookies in her other hand. When she smiled at them, he didn't think she looked all that happy to be summoned to them.

"I was in the middle of a meeting with some of the other magical creatures that help me keep up with the world. I do hope that whatever you need is important...never mind. The meeting wasn't going the way that I wanted it, so I'm happy for the intrusion. What is it I can do for the two of you?" Loman turned around and showed her his back. Lindsley did the same. Her face went from looking mild annoyance to surprise and embarrassment in seconds. "Oh my goodness, I didn't tell you about them. Oh, Loman and Lindsley, I am profoundly sorry for that. You must...I was going to say that you must forgive me, but you shouldn't. I should have let you know. I'm sure you have a great many questions about why they're here."

"I do. We both do. They're under our skin, Andonna. Under. Our. Skin." She laughed, and he felt his anger surge up a great deal more than he thought he'd ever been before. "This is not a laughing matter. What the fuck is happening to us?"

"Let me give you…no, that would take too long. Here, let me give it all to you at once." She only touched her fingers to their heads, and he fell back on the sofa behind him. His head felt like it was going to explode. "You're going to be just fine, both of you. Just let it sort around for you, and you'll know all there is to know about having my fae helping you."

Loman woke in his bed with Lindsley beside him. She was on her phone, talking to who sounded like her sister. Once she noticed that he was awake or conscious, it was difficult to know right now. She told Andi that she'd call her back later. Once she put her phone away, she turned to him.

"We were given a download on this shit. That's the only way that I can describe it." He asked her what she'd figured out. "Everything. I mean, that's not really true. I've figured out that when I need information on anything, it's right there for me to, I guess, sort of upload like where something is on a computer. I just have to ask myself what I need to know, and it's right there. Also, Mitar is able to retrieve anything that I need, like you too. If you're out on a site, and you need, I don't know, extra film or something, she can get it for you. Or extra blankets. Whatever you need."

"I can see where that would be helpful. But film? I've not used film in a decade. But I do understand what you're talking about. I can almost feel that the information for anything that I want is right on the tip of my tongue." She said that she's already had Mitar help with some of the projects that she has going on at the gallery. Like the need for more display items. "Good. I guess you'd have to tell him what you're looking for, and he produces it? Or does he go out and find it?"

"Both. If he can replicate something that I need, then he will. But if it's something that he doesn't understand, then he'll go and find something like it, and we'll work from there. Also, and this is something that we have to get used to. They have to connect with us daily, like they did today, so that they can be in sync with us. Know all the things that we've been thinking about." Loman asked about sex. "I've not broached that subject yet. We'll have to figure that one out as we go. I've already told both of them that the bedroom is off-limits unless we call out for them. I don't want them around when we go to bed."

"I love that idea. Yes, it would just be too much to be coming out of the shower, and there they are." He knew other things that they could do for them too. "Like fixing our car should be stranded."

They talked about all the different things that could be helpful with the fae around. The two got up and made their way downstairs to find the two faes in the kitchen. Meggie, Lindsley's mom, was there talking to the little people. She seemed less freaked out about them than he had.

"They were just telling me that I need to have a fae with me too. I'm not so sure that I'd like to have to worry about someone else right now. I'm on the mend, sure, but I don't want to let someone down right now." She smiled at him. "Loman, dear, my ex-husband, the murdering son of a bitch would like to talk to me. I was wondering if you could go there to the jail and set him straight. Or murder him. I don't care which right now. But the thought of you having to go to jail makes me think I need to put up with him until he—hopefully, sooner rather than later—dies of old age. The man is nothing but a pain in my backside."

"I can do that for you, no problem. In fact, I'll go this morning and get it over with. I have some work that I have to pick up for my brothers, so it'll be no trouble for me to go there and see him." She thanked him. "I hope that you and Andi are settling in all right. My mom said that the two of you had lunch yesterday and that she enjoyed herself very much."

"Your mother is a hoot, I don't mind saying, but I like her very much. She can cut you to the quick without raising her voice and never use a single curse word. I just love that about her. And that grandda of yours? I'd love to just bundle him up and keep him around for getting me out of a funk. He seems to know when I am in one too." Nodding, Loman told her that he more than likely did know. "He's a sweetheart and a better man than I've ever met. It's easy to see where you boys got all your charm too. He's a charmer, that one."

"He's always been a charmer. When he was in trouble with my grandma, he'd go out of his way to make it up to her. Grandda didn't do things by halves either. When he was in trouble, every shop in town would be in the black by the end of the day." They all laughed. "Grandma, she really would have loved all the women in this family. And the children here? My goodness, she would have been right on the ground with them when they played outside too."

Loman ate a sandwich with the women in his life and headed to the jail, enjoying it the entire time. Amerdan followed along with him, peppering him with questions about Allen all the way there. Getting things set up with the men on duty, he made his way back to the cells to see what the hell the man wanted now.

~*~

Allen didn't care for being in jail. Although he didn't think that anyone would enjoy being locked up with the minimal amount of getting what he wanted. He shouldn't be here. It was his family's fault. Once

Loman was seated across from him, asking him how things were going, he wanted to come through the bars and knock the ever-loving shit out of him. When he mentioned that he was his son-in-law now, Allen didn't believe him.

"None of my daughters would stoop so low as to marry while I'm rotting away in here. I didn't even get an invite to the wedding either. And I know for a fact that it would have been a lavish wedding with the kind of money — well, the kind that I used to have before they stole it all from me. No, I won't believe it." Loman told him that he didn't care if he did or didn't. "You're very uppity, aren't you, young man? Well, since my wife won't come to see me, I'm going to have to depend on you to get things rolling in the right direction so that I can get back to my gallery. You're going to do that too. If, in fact, we're now related."

"No. I'm not doing shit for you. And it was never your gallery, Allen, but Meggie's. And just so you're aware, they've made some wonderful changes to the place. When the grand opening happens, it will draw in a great many people. But the best part is, every one of the artists will get their money too." Allen asked him if he was stupid. "I'm not. However, if you think that you're ever going to get out of here for any other reason than going to prison, then you're stupid. You tried to kill your wife. Not to mention all the money you stole and thought you could keep by stashing it away overseas. That's mail fraud, you idiot. Then there is the stolen artwork that was found in the storage unit that was in your name. Is there any low that you won't stoop to?"

"She didn't die, now did she? Besides, if I had wanted her dead, she'd be dead. I just wanted to scare her a little. There isn't any harm in a man taking his wife to task when she does what she did to me, as for Mail fraud. I didn't mail a single thing through the mailbox. I did it all online. Now, who's the idiot. You have to put a stamp on something for it to be called mail. Did you know that she and my daughters took all my money and gave it away? That nearly had me having a heart attack. I'm going to have to talk to them about not touching things that don't belong to them." Loman asked him if he thought it was all right that he didn't kill his wife. "Of course, it's not all right. But I got her attention, didn't I? Besides, she deserved it for treating me the way—did you know they took away my credit cards too? And not only did they empty my bank accounts out without my permission, but they also took all my stash money from me. I'm going to be able to get all that back, too, when my family gets the rod out of their collective asses and let me out of here. I want you to talk to Meggie and tell her that I want her to drop the charges against me that I tried to kill her. As I said, she's not dead, and that should make her happy. Also, since we're related, I want you to find me a good attorney too. I'm going to sue Meggie once I'm out of here. My daughters too."

"You just don't get it, do you? You're not going to get out of here." He said he was if he would do what he told him to do. "In the event that it hasn't crossed your mind yet, I'm not going to find you an attorney, as I'm helping my brother Cass file a large suit against you for all the shit that you've done in the name of making you wealthy. You're also in trouble with the IRS for not reporting the income you stole from the artist you were supposed to be helping. And if I have my way about it, you're going to be charged with the death of David Windermere in his suicide because you robbed him of not just his work that you sold off but the money that should have gone to him. You're a piece of shit."

"I'm a man trying to make it in this world. Unlike you, everything wasn't handed to me on a silver platter, young man." He said that he's worked hard for his money. "Sure you did. By taking pretty pictures? I no more believe that than I do that you're married to my daughter. Which one is it, by the way? Andi? Lindsley? I doubt that you'd get Lindsley to say yes. She's nothing but a workaholic. I shouldn't have allowed her to go to college. Though now that I think on it, I'm not even positive that they went. But something made her uppity. But then, I guess the two of you are well suited if it's her. Which one? Not that I'm going to believe you either way."

Loman stood up, and he told him to sit down. He wasn't finished with him yet. Instead of doing what he told him, he came closer to the bars. When he reached out his hand, Allen thought for sure that he was going to shake his hand, tell him that he had his back in this. Instead, after taking his hand, he fucking clawed him with what appeared to be a large lion's paw.

The cut wasn't deep, but it was painful. Even as he started to bleed, his blood dripping to the floor, Loman spoke. When he didn't hear him, his body still in shock from what he'd done, he jerked him to the bars and told him to pay attention.

"Are you listening to me now?" Nodding, Allen said that he was hurting him. "You're going to be hurting a good deal more if you ever call my home again. I will come here and destroy you so that they'll be cleaning bits and pieces of you out of this cell for the rest of my life. Which is going to be a hell of a lot longer than you're going to be alive. Stay away from my family, Allen. That would include Meggie, Andi and Lindsley. Or so help me, I'm going to put such a hurt on you that you're never going to recover from."

"Did you just threaten me? Mother fucker, I'm not someone that you should be fucking around with. Do you hear me? Let me the fuck go." He was shoved across the cell, where his head hit the wall behind him. Sliding down the wall because the pain made him weak in the knees, he sat there. Stunned to the point where he was seeing double, he couldn't get his mouth to work. Sliding to his left, he hit his head a second time on his commode. Christ, nothing was going according to the way he wanted right now.

When he woke up, he was in some kind of curtained-off room. Listening to the things going on over the loudspeaker, Allen figured out that he was in the hospital. Raising his head up, he puked all over himself when the pain in his head made him sick. A nurse was suddenly in front of him, telling him that he was going to get stitched up soon.

"That man, Loman, something Foster, he hurt me. Threatened me too. I want to press charges against him. My wife and daughters—he never did tell me which one of my stupid daughters he thinks he's married to either." She told him to shut his mouth about the Fosters. "I will not. Damn it all to fuck and back. Doesn't anyone care that I don't want to be in jail? I need to get home to make some more money. Christ ole mighty, I fucking hate everyone right now."

"The Fosters have donated a great deal of money to this hospital, and you'd better watch yourself in saying that you want them arrested." He was going to sock her in the mouth when he realized that he was cuffed to the bed like he was some kind of animal. He even told her about Loman being some kind of lion. "We all know that, dummy. Loman's brother is the king of all lions. You don't get around much, do you? I suppose it's because you've been trying to kill off your lovely wife. She's a good woman and deserves better than you. I'm glad that she was granted a divorce from the likes of you."

"You don't know what you're talking about. And I'll tell her when she's divorced or not." That made more sense in his head, but right now, he wanted out of there. "Look, I'll slip you some cash if you just look the other way and let me go. Fifty bucks should do that, don't you think? You can buy yourself a nice new haircut with that much. I don't know what you've done to your hair, lady, but it's not a look for you."

When she left him lying there, without so much as an idea when he was getting out, the doctor came in and said he was going to stitch him up. Allen asked him if he was going to give him something to knock him out.

"I'm not, as a matter of fact. Linda, the nurse that you just insulted, said that you didn't deserve anything. So brace yourself, Mr. Benson. This is going to hurt."

He didn't believe he'd be so cruel as to actually stitch him up without so much as an aspirin to take away the pain. Didn't he have to take some kind of oath saying that he'd not stitch someone up like this? Something about no harm to humans. The first time he stuck the needle in his head, Allen screamed in pain.

Fifteen stitches. He had to have fifteen stitches to put his head back in one piece. Allen was sure that he was just stabbing him with the needle when he was finished up so that he'd be in more pain. Not only had he pissed himself, but he was sick again with the pain of it. And he'd sweat like a hog out in the sun all day. If they'd not had him chained down, he would have killed the mother fucking doctor.

They wouldn't give him anything for the pain even after they were finished making him suffer like they had. Once he was fit to go, they told him he'd be taken back to his cell and given something for the pain. He had a feeling that whatever it was, they weren't going to give him anything good. Probably some expired drug that didn't work when they invented it.

It took them what felt like an hour to get him cleaned up after he'd made a mess of himself. There wasn't any way that he was going to make it until next week before he was able to shower again. No amount of begging would even get him a wet cloth so that he could at least not be sick to his belly every time he smelled himself.

If he had some paper and pencil, he'd be making a list of the shit storm that he was going to be bringing down on some heads when he was out of jail. And he would be too. They didn't have shit on him after Meggie did her duty by him and dropped the charges she'd pressed about him not killing her. After all, it wasn't his fault anyway. She was the one that kicked him to the curb. Literally too.

Thinking about how he was going to be able to generate some sympathy for himself, he thought about the newspaper. He hadn't any idea if this town had a daily rag or not. But he knew there were big names he could call in a couple of favors for. When Meggie gave him control of the gallery, which is what he'd be getting returned to him soon, she also gave him a list of phone numbers for the large newspapers around the country. He'd never used them before, and not wanting to spend money on advertising when he could just pocket it on his own, he decided that he was going to do it now. All he had to do was get one of his daughters to bring him the list. Christ, they'd better too. He'd beat them if they tried the shit on him that they'd been doing lately.

By the time he was back in his cell, he was sicker than ever. His head was pounding, and he was nearly sick to his belly every time he moved. Just lying on the cot that he hated, Allen begged for what seemed like hours for someone to come give him the promised medication.

"I've brought you some food. You can't take the medication without food in your stomach. It's dangerous, it says here." He told the guard that he was just too sick for anything to stay down. "Then you can't have anything for the pain. I don't care one way or the other, but I have to make sure you eat something before I can give you this."

"This is just ridiculous. Why can't I, for once, have my own way about something? Why is it always everyone else that is making the rules that I'm supposed to follow?" The guard didn't say anything, but he did laugh. "Laugh it up, kid. Once I'm out of here, I'm going to be making sure that all of you are out of a job."

He was able to keep down a handful of chips and two bites of the cheese sandwich that was with it. Not the best choice of food, he discovered later when he threw up the chips and the undigested sandwich and the medication. He was tempted to rinse them off and take them again. By golly, he was going to do it too.

After dragging his ass to the sink with the nasty-looking drugs cupped in his hand, he rinsed them off, careful of not making them too melty and the drug not working. He'd done that once, and he'd been sick. Back then, he'd cut the medication up into smaller doses so that he could get them down better. That lasted only long enough for him to get back to his bed before it all came up again.

Taking the medication as soon as he cleaned them off, he laid back on the cot so that he could get his head to stop hurting. The pills seemed to be working a little for him, and he was glad that he'd been able to outsmart someone today. He was going to mark this up as a win for himself and not think of the rest of the day's shit show.

He was just dozing off when he felt his chest hurting. It didn't bother him so much now that he was feeling less pain than before. Even as his body started to numb up, taking him under, Allen had a finger of fear that he'd made an error in judgement about the medication that he had taken without food.

Chapter 6

He's had to have emergency surgery. The medication that he took, without food, it seems, caused him to have a massive stroke. Right now, they're hoping that they'll be able to repair some of the damage that was caused." Meggie asked him why he'd been given the medication without food. "The guard made him eat some food when he handed over the pills. The cameras in his cell showed him getting sick. Then like an idiot, he rinsed off the two pills and took them again. Since they were already activated, for lack of a better term, once they hit his system, it was what caused his heart to fail. I'm sorry."

Loman held onto Andi while she cried. She had told him before he'd left to see her dad that she was going to go and talk to him later today. However, that didn't happen because he'd been in the ER, and then he'd been taken to the hospital again for the head injuries.

"You said that you cut him. I'm not sorry that you did it. The very fact that he drove you, a very calm and laid-back person, tells me that it was all his fault. Dad could get on a person's last nerve after dancing on the others while he was trying to make a point." He thought that Lindsley knew her father better than anyone, including Meggie. When she told him that he'd more than likely blame everyone for what happened to him, Loman thought she was correct. "We're going to have to make provisions for where he's going to be staying until he is to the point where he can take care of himself."

"A nursing home?" Lindsley told her mom that she thought that might be the best place for him. "What if he isn't able to ever care for himself again? The doctor said that was a good possibility too. Will we have to find one for the long term?"

Parker and Don joined them in the waiting room. His family had been taking turns staying with him and the other Bensons since Allen had been brought in. They'd bring in food and drinks or just sit and talk to them about how things were going with the things around town. Distraction was working well for all of them, he thought. Especially Meggie.

Meggie had been married to Allen for thirty-one years. Loman overheard her telling his mom that she hadn't any idea why she had married Allen. She didn't think that she ever loved him. But she had gotten two of the best daughters out of the deal. Meggie thought that she got the better end of the deal.

"He's always been like he is, then?" Meggie said he'd not been as obvious about his need to be a prick. "Sounds like he got used to having things his own way and just let himself stop hiding it from people when no one took him to task. Now that you have, he's blaming it all on you three. The nurse at the hospital, when he went in for stitches, said that he'd told her he was sick of nothing going his way anymore. She thought that he sounded like a selfish child."

"I think that describes him the best. He's more

than selfish, but childlike is just what he is." Lindsley laid her head on his shoulder as she continued. "I've had very little to do with him since leaving home. Then we heard about the suicide, and I knew something was wrong with the gallery. It was Andi that started the investigation, and she brought mom and me on board when she found that he'd been stealing from the company and us. The really funny part is we told him what we were going to do and gave him a month to get his shit together. He didn't think we'd do it from what I figured out."

"As I said, he'd been getting away with stuff for a long time and decided that he could tell you to back off, and you would. Allen won't be happy if he's in a nursing home either, I'm betting." Meggie laughed and said that she might just find him the worse one there was and put him in there for all that he'd done to them. "If you don't mind, I'll have my sisters look into finding him someplace. I'll have them look for both, good and bad."

Meggie laughed again and then started crying. It was grandda that held her while she sobbed on his shoulder. She was telling him that she'd been a terrible person for thinking such a thing about the man she'd been married to. Grandda assured her that they all had bad thoughts about people like that from time to time, and it was a good thing to be able to get things like that off one's chest.

The surgeon came to talk to them about two hours later. Since Meggie said it was all right for all the family to be there, he sat down to tell them what he'd been able to do for Allen. He looked grim, and that was very telling, he thought.

"The stroke was devastating to his body. Right now, I'm not entirely sure what sort of bodily damage has been done to him. We can only wait until he wakes up and shows us what kind of things will need to be dealt with." Meggie asked if he'd be paralyzed. "I would like to tell you that he won't be, but I think with the damage, as I said, he'll be at least partially paralyzed. That was showing when he came in."

"How long will it be before we know anything?" Loman held onto Lindsley's hand as the doctor thought about his answer. "I'm not going to hold you to anything you tell us. But since my parents are divorced, we'll, as a family, need to make plans for his convalescence."

"He'll need to have constant care at the beginning. When I say that, I want you to understand that he's going to need to be able to work with people in order to keep himself fit enough to live as long as he can. Do you think he'll be all right with that? I'm sorry to say this because I know it's cruel, but from what I've heard, he's never been very cooperative with anyone."

"No, he's not. That's why we need to find him a place that will not just work with him but not take any of his bullshit." Andi stood up. "I have to go to work. I can't sit around here any longer waiting on answers. Mom, will you go and have lunch with me? All of you can join us if you wish. I just don't want mom sitting around here either thinking of things she should have or shouldn't have done concerning our father."

When Andi said she was headed to the bathroom first, the doctor looked at all of them. With a huge smile, he said that, as a family, they should let that young lady fix up her father's care. She'd be the best for it because she has the balls to make him get better no matter what he wants.

"I think you're right about that." When the doctor left them, the rest of them gathered up their things. Before leaving, Loman made sure that they had his number to call if something happened. Since he knew all the staff from his family helping with projects concerning the hospital, he felt better about knowing that he was leaving Allen in good hands. No matter how much he wouldn't appreciate it.

Lunch was a somber affair. It wasn't as if they were totally upset with the way he was sure they felt about Allen but that there was the unknown. Was he going to be able to care for himself? From what he thought, the doctor was telling them that he'd be able to, but would he want to. He looked at Parker when she sat down next to Meggie.

"I can make him well. I would do that for all of you. I cannot change him, not his way of doing things but making him well enough to be able to get around. I can do that." Meggie asked her what it would cost her. She said that she knew a couple of lesser witches. "You're a wonderful person Meggie for asking, but there would be no trouble for me to do this for you. You're family, and I would do this for you no matter the trouble that might come back on me."

"You're saying that you could make him healthy

again? A full recovery?" Parker told Andi she'd do that, too, if that was their wish. "I guess I don't understand what it is you're telling me. I'm, along with my sister and mom or the rip the fucking bandage off and tell me what it is you're not telling us."

"All right. I'm better at that, anyway. I could make your father make a full recovery. Like nothing at all happened. I'd rather not only because I know that he'd only go back to his own ways of getting back at the three of you. Perhaps even Loman in some way. Or I could make it so that while he'd not be able to get around without a wheelchair or some other device to walk to get around. It's up to you. However, and this is something that you need to think about. Will whatever you do for him make you happy. I don't want to do this because you're feeling guilty about him being in the position he put himself in and want him to be better. I can almost taste your guilt, and not one thing that has happened to him is any of your faults. He was told several times that he needed to take the drug with food. He didn't. Allen thought that he was smarter than any doctor around." Meggie asked if she knew what was going to happen to Allen should they do nothing. "He'll be bedridden. He won't be able to talk or go to the bathroom, nor will he be able to eat solid foods. The stroke affected his brain severely, and he'll never recover from it. Again, this is all on him."

"You say that because you know that I'm going to be able to live with myself with the results of his stroke. I'm not asking you to take away my pain. But can you tell me what he'll be like if you help him out?" Parker only laid her hand on Meggie's head. Loman reached over and took her hand into his, hoping to give her comfort in whatever Parker was doing for her. He was able to see what she was too.

With a full recovery, he was just as Parker said, still trying to get the family to give him back his job, and he pestered Meggie so much that in the end, she asked to have her immortality taken away, and she committed suicide. Loman's heart hurt worse than he'd ever felt before when he stood with his wife when they found her.

The second option of him being able to get around with a wheelchair was just as bad. He not only pestered them for his job, but when he saw his family, especially Meggie, he would run her down with his wheelchair when she tried to ignore him. Sabotage the gallery. Hurt his wife and sister-in-law. It was too much. Removing her hand from Meggie's head, he looked at Parker and asked her if it was an unchangeable future.

"It will be set in stone if I change him, yes." He looked at Lindsley, then at Meggie. He could tell that she was upset about the actions of her ex-husband. When she looked at Parker, she straightened up her back and looked at her. "You've come to a decision, then."

"I have. Don't waste your magic on him. He's not worth it. And if I ever come to you about my immortality, I want you to show me the face on my child's face when she finds my body." Parker assured her that she'd do that but also told her that she'd never ask for that again. "Thank you for that. And I thank you for what you've told me about Allen. I love you for that, Parker. And your honesty about it."

"Thank you for that too, Meggie. You're a good person that doesn't need to saddle yourself down with such a monster." When Parker disappeared, it was Don that explained why she'd left so abruptly.

"She's not good with compliments. My darling

wife handles criticism better than she does when someone tells her what a good person she is." Loman laughed, and so did Lindsley. But Meggie told him to let Parker know she was going to be doing it a great deal more. She was going to have to deal with it. Don laughed with the rest of them.

They didn't hear from the hospital by the time they headed back to his house. Meggie was going to take a nap. It had been too stressful for her. And Andi was going to go shopping. She had things that she wanted to put in her rooms.

He and Lindsley decided to sit on the couch and watch a little television. There really wasn't anything on, but it was just boring enough to put them both to sleep. It was nearly midnight when he got a call from the hospital. Allen was awake enough to know what they'd be dealing with, he was told.

"It's not a good outcome, Loman." He told the nurse they'd be right in. "Good. You hold onto that family you have, hun. You have yourself a good one there."

"I know that. I'm going to hold onto them forever if they let me." He woke up Meggie and Andi. Told them what the nurse had told him. Andi, he figured, had written off her father long ago and opted to stay home. Since she knew the outcome, she would rather stay here than to see him like that.

As soon as they entered the ward Allen was in, he could see that everyone was expecting them to be terribly upset. When Meggie hugged the nurse that had called, it was visible that everyone thought that they were going to be just fine. Even after talking with the doctor about Allen's prognosis, Meggie and Lindsley seemed to be ready to make the arrangements that would get him the best care while he was alive. He hadn't asked, but Meggie did, how long would Allen live in the state that he was in now.

"I would say with very good care, he might be able to live for another year or two. I wouldn't think much longer than that. His organs were damaged by the medication. His kidneys and liver are not functioning to full capacity." Meggie thanked him. "I have to say, Meggie, that you're taking this a great deal better than I think most would. And I'm going to say that it's because you have all this support. Lean on the Fosters, and they'll make even the worse kind of news better to deal with."

"I have been. And I'm going to continue to do so. All right, doctor, can you recommend a couple of places where we can set up for Allen?" He said that he'd have his nurse talk to her. "Good. Once he's out of the hospital, I want him to be able to go directly to someplace right away. I don't like leaving things to chance. Thank you for all you did for my family."

"My pleasure." The doctor looked at him. "I want to thank you as well, Loman. Your family has made it possible for this hospital to remain afloat and have the best equipment. Thank you all for that."

~*~

Lindsley went home that night feeling better than she had in a good long time. It wasn't just having the best husband in the world, though, that helped a great deal. She was also getting things set up for their future with the gallery.

"I've found an auction house that will go the extra mile in selling off the gems that you have. I told him there were quite a few of them, and he said he thought you should dole them out slowly. Maybe have two dozen of them for sale, then in a few months, have another sale. I think I kind of like that idea." Loman had been going to different auction houses for the last few days to find them the best place. "Also, since there will be no names attached to the sale, he said we could be there if we wanted to see how things go. I was assured that since they're uncut gems, they won't be worth as much as the cut ones, but I don't think you'd care about that, do you?"

"Parker told me that she could cut them for us. Polish this up so that they're worth hundreds to thousands of dollars more. I'm not greedy about it, but it would be nice since my grandda saved them for us to get the best possible price." She smiled at him. "Even Andonna said that she could fix them all with a sweep of her hand. Either way that would get us the best price."

He agreed with her and then got down on one knee before her. She asked him what he was doing. Smiling, he told her to hush up.

"Meggie let me pick out any gem that I wanted. All I could think about when I saw the array of all the beautiful gems, they didn't compare to your beauty." Lindsley couldn't help it. She started crying softly.

"If you do that, I'm going to think you don't want to marry me."

"I do. So very much. I've been saying that we're married to everyone. The thought of making it real? Well, I love you, Loman Foster. Please make me Lindsley Foster too." He slipped the ring on her finger, up to her knuckle. "Oh, Loman, it's beautiful. I loved the moonstone when I saw it."

It was beautiful too. The heart-shaped moonstone was surrounded by smaller diamonds. The band was wide and made of what appeared to be gold. There were gold bands over the heart that held it in place. Once she had the ring on her finger, Loman stood up and pulled her into his arms. It was a place where she thought she could live forever. When he kissed her, she felt the earth move under her feet, and her heart sing with happiness.

"I want to have children with you." He told her that anytime she was ready, he'd try very hard to make it happen. "Not too hard, please. The last time you nearly killed me. Maybe you should try just a little less and make a baby or twelve with me."

"Anything you want, my dear. I will spend my

entire life making you happy." They went through the information that the auctioneer gave them. Calling for Andonna to help with the gems, she literally did wave her hand over the gems that they'd brought home and made them not just polished up, but they were cut beautifully. She said that the others in the boxes at the bank were finished too. Then she sat down on the couch when asked to.

"I have something that I'd like to talk over with you." Andonna asked her if she was going to send the fae back to her. "No. Not at all. I've come to rely on Mitar and Amerdan very much. They don't help Loman as much as they do me, but we're all right with that as well. No, this is about your realm. I was thinking that I'd like to send my mother there for a little while. If you would allow it. She's very stressed, and I think that she could use a little magic to help her."

"She's never been there before. I've asked her, but she said that she has much too much to do to go and sit with her feet up. I don't know why she'd think I'd allow her to do that, but I would so love for her to come there. How long were you thinking?" Lindsley said that it would be up to her on how long she could stand her. "I would make her a permanent resident if she'd allow it. Even having a home for her to come to when she visits me."

"If you make that happen, I'll make sure that she comes with her bags packed. I wouldn't want her around here when it's time to move my father. I think that would be hard on her." Andonna looked at Loman. "This was his idea. He thinks that once my mom sees a unicorn, she'll never want to leave."

"She can ride one if it pleases her. I know it will my special ponies." Andonna clapped her hands and then hugged her. "She'll need no luggage to bring. The faeries and fae will be so happy to have someone to take care of that they'll be begging to be a part of her crew. Oh, the things that the two of us will be up to."

"Then it's settled. My father is going to be moved to the nursing home in three days. They've done all they can for him at the hospital, and they need the bed. I'd like to have her there either tonight or tomorrow, so she doesn't have to be here, as I said." Andonna said that she'd be ready for her. "Two things. My mom is a diabetic. Not many people know that, so she'll need to—"

"Once she became an immortal, honey, she no longer was anything but a healthy, happy woman." Lindsley said she'd not thought to ask about that. Then asked Loman if thyroid medication was necessary. "No. I'm sorry that I didn't mention this before. That is my fault. No, once you became a part of this family, all ailments and anything that you might have had, like cancer, just simply disappeared. I'm sorry, honey."

"I just thought of something. Andi, will she be able to have children? When she was younger, they told her that her womb was damaged. I don't remember what they said now, but it was clear she'd not be able to carry a baby to term. She could get pregnant, but she'd never be able to carry one for long. Will she now?" Loman told her that if nothing had been removed, then he didn't think that she'd have an issue. "I have to get her to a doctor. Today if I can. Do you know one? Of course, you do. You know — I have to call her."

When she was finally able to get in touch with her sister, Andi was terrified to find the information out. But after talking to Parker for a little while, she assured them both that Andi was as fit as anyone when it came to her having as many children as she wanted.

They were all so happy they danced around the room for a good twenty minutes, crying and laughing at the same time.

"Just to be sure, it's not that I don't believe Parker, but I'd like to just go to the doctor. Then when he tells me that I'm perfectly fine, I want to punch him in the nuts for being so cruel to me when he told me I'd be a motherless woman for the rest of my life." Parker asked her if he'd really said that to her. "Yes. The fucking prick. He even told me that most men wouldn't want to marry someone that couldn't give them what they wanted, and that was a child. I've been…it's been hurting me since he told me. I've lived my life for the last ten years pushing men away because of his terrible words to me then."

"I'll take care of him." Both Andi her herself told Parker not to kill him. "Oh, all right. Everyone says that to me. I wonder where they got the idea that I kill people all the time. But I'll only make him regret it. After I do a little research on him. I want to find out if he's done this to other women. I, for one, wouldn't want him working as a physician if he's going to be that horrific to people. There is no reason for that." She winked at them. "I'll be right back."

When she disappeared, Andi looked at her. "She won't kill him, will she? I mean, she's a wonderful person, and I love her to pieces, but she can be a little intense when she's upset about something." Lindsley said that she's protective of her family. "Yes, well, how will I find someone to love me if she goes around killing off men that upset me. I think she might. I would be like a black widow or something if it ever comes out that men die after breaking it off with me."

When Parker returned, she was laughing so hard that it was difficult for her to get the story out. Apparently, when she arrived at this office, he was fucking one of his patients to give her his child. The woman wasn't even awake when he was doing this. So the police raided his office, catching him with his pants down around his ankles.

"I got the police there right away, and when they found him there, they were shocked beyond doing anything until he was finished." Parker laughed again. "My god, you should have seen his face when the women in the lobby found him there with the tiniest dick I've ever seen on a man. It's no wonder he could do that to women. It's doubtful that they felt a thing. I swear to you ladies, he was smaller than a tampon."

Lindsley thought she'd laugh about that for decades. To think that without any effort much on their part, the man was going to go to prison. And knowing that her sister would be able to be a mom was so much better than anything that she could have hoped for.

Chapter 7

Getting up to go to the bathroom, Loman stood in front of the mirror for several minutes after finishing up and washing his hands. Yesterday had been a horrific day. Allen had been taken to a nursing home in Cincinnati where he'd get the best care money could buy, and Meggie and her daughters had decided not to go to see to his care at the last minute. It wasn't until the ambulance left that Meggie started having doubts about her decision to go. Lindsley stayed back with her sister Andi who was suddenly taking it hard that her dad was gone.

"What are you doing up so early? Big plans?"

Lindsley leaned against his back and kissed his shoulder. "Mom called me just now. She's on her way here from the grocery store. I hate to say this, but she's making me crazy with all these whiny things she is worrying about dad. She wants me to take her down there in a few days to make sure that he's in good hands. She sounds a good deal better than she did last night, but that's not to say that in a few minutes, she's going to be blaming herself for dad's health issues right now. Mom said that he'd done this all on his own, and she wasn't going to live with the consequences that took him where he is now. At least right now, she is. I find myself avoiding her, so I don't have to be mean and tell her to get over it. What do you think?"

"I think you're right. I can talk to her if you want. If she could remember that every time she feels bad because he's in a nursing home. I love your mom, and I'm so sorry for her feelings over this. I just wish there was something that I could do to help her. Andi, I guess she's taking this pretty hard as well." Lindsley pulled away from him, and he turned around. "Did I say something wrong?"

"No, not at all. I was just thinking that you

needed me to suck on your cock until you come." He couldn't have been more shocked than he was at that moment. "Unless you don't want me to. I can get into the shower and—"

He jerked her toward him and kissed her. Reaching down to the bottom of her nightgown, he wasn't surprised to find her pantiless and wet. Sliding his fingers into her curls, he moaned when she spread her legs wider for him. When she pulled back a little, nibbling on his lower lip until it slipped from her mouth.

"I want to suck on your cock, big boy. And have you come down my throat. Then when we finish with that, I want you to lean me over the sink and fuck me until I hurt." Christ, Loman thought, Lindsley was going to kill him.

Sliding down his body, she took his boxer briefs with her. His cock was caught on the elastic at one point, and she used her teeth to free him. Even with her pulling his briefs off his legs, she was sliding her tongue around the crown of his cock so nicely that he closed his eyes and leaned back against the sink and mirror.

He'd never been a big fan of having his cock blown. But Christ, right now, he was sure that he'd never feel the same way about it again. The way that Lindsley cupped his balls in her warm palm. She rolled them gently so as not to cause him pain but the biggest thrill that he could endure.

Her mouth was a wizard of ecstasy and pain. Lindsley's teeth scraped gently down his cock, taking small nips until she reached his balls. There she would take them into her mouth, one at a time and lave them with her tongue. Loman was so close to coming so many times that he was sure that his heart was going to burst in his chest the way it would pound.

Fucking her mouth, Loman tried to be as gentle as he could. But the moment his cock slid past the tightness at the back of her throat, he came hard enough to make his eyes roll to the back of his head. His toes curled under his feet painfully. And when she cupped his balls again, it was all he could do not to pull her head to him and fuck her hard.

When she pulled her mouth free of his cock, he heard a small pop sound. While he didn't know why it was a huge turn-on for her to make that sound, he picked her up from the floor and did just what she wanted him to do. Pressing her body over the sink, he slammed his still-hard cock in her from behind and fucked her pussy as hard as she wanted.

Watching her breast swing in the mirror made him hurt. Reaching up with one hand, he filled it with her lovely breast and squeezed. Her cries of enjoyment encouraged him to continue to play with her breast, and then he tweaked her nipple. Loman had never had such enjoyment in fucking someone before. Lifting her up so that she could see herself in the mirror, he slid his hand down to her pussy and pushed his thumb into her clit and watched her as she screamed through the most volatile climax he'd ever seen.

Fucking her again, he nearly missed coming inside of her. When she, weak from coming so hard, leaned over, he let go of himself and filled her deeply with his cum. Loman could feel the hurt and pull of his muscles when he came again. If they continued to try and outdo each other, he wasn't going to make it to eternity. Immortality was going to be the only thing that would save him at this point.

Lindsley was out when he picked her up. Putting

her back in the bed, he staggered to the other side of it and sat down. He had a lot to do today, and right now, all he wanted to do was climb back into his bed and never wake. Getting up, dizzy with the quick movement, Loman decided that he needed a long hot shower.

By the time he'd run out of hot water, he felt better. Getting dressed, he quietly made his way downstairs. Meggie was in the kitchen with their new cook going over some of the things she wanted to try now that she was no longer a diabetic. He found Andi on a dating app. That tickled him to no end.

"You do know that there are any number of people around town that would give you their everything if you were to consent to go on a date with them. And some of the people that work for Brook, if you don't mind dating ex-cons drool every time you come around a job site they're on." She said she didn't mind dating ex-cons. She knew that they'd paid their debt. "Good for you. If you really are serious about just dating a few men for fun, I'd suggest you do something for me to meet a few. The pack leader here is looking to expand his contact with the outside world. His name is Jonah Marks, and he's only just taken over the pack. Then there is the pride that is nearby. I think his name is Denver Tucker. They're the group that is moving out to California soon. Anyway, if you'd go out there and meet with his committee and see what they want, I'm sure by the time you're ready to leave, there will be any number of men ready to take you anywhere you want to go."

"I'm sure that will not happen. But I will go out and talk to him. If you'd let him know that I'm coming, that would be wonderful. Oh, the fliers for the gallery's grand opening have been sent to the printers. I'm so glad that I had people look over it for mistakes. Can you imagine how stupid we would have looked if Brook hadn't caught that we spelled our last name wrong? Sheesh." He said he'd make the call now. "Thank you, Loman. For everything. Not just this call that I'm making. You've gone the extra mile for all of us, and I couldn't love you any more than if you were by biological brother."

He kissed her on the forehead and then handed the phone to her. When she smiled at him and took the house phone to the other room, Loman did his best to get Meggie in a better mood. Finally, he just told her she needed a break and sent her outside. It was hard for him to treat the older woman that way, but she was nitpicking him to death about the nursing home where Allen was.

"You're treating me like I'm a child." He asked her if she thought that she was acting like one. "I don't, but apparently, you do. I'm worried about his care."

"Why? Do you think that you worrying about it will make it any better or less? Do you suppose he cares if you worry about him?" He knew that he was being mean, but she was even driving his mom nuts about this. "Let me ask you something, Meggie. Do you suppose that if he were awake and able to get around, he'd be picking you to death over things? He would, and you know it. He'd be wanting better food even though it is rated the best in the state. Allen would want to be catered to every moment. And he'd be calling all of you wondering when you're going to be getting him back at his job. He can't do that because he was stupid and thought he was smarter than anyone else. I'm not doing this to make you feel terrible. But you're driving a wedge between you and your daughters for no reason whatsoever. I swear to you, when my sisters looked for the best for him, he got it. And we didn't do it for him. We did this for you and your daughters so that you'd not have to worry all the time. He's where he needs to be, and he'll get whatever he needs to be as comfortable as they can make him. So that you don't have to worry all the time. You're stressing yourself out for no reason."

"He was my husband, and I hated him." When she sobbed and held onto him when she told him the real reason she was upset, he suddenly understood. "I never loved him. Never. He was just a means to get my daughters. That's all. And when I let him run the gallery, it was getting him away from me. I wanted him out of my life, and I figured that if he fucked up enough, pardon my language that I'd have a good reason to get him out of my life. But he tried to kill me. Then he was foolish enough—just as you said to get himself where he is today. I feel guilty, Loman. I never meant for him to be hurt when I divorced him. I just didn't want him around me anymore."

"You didn't do anything. Not one thing to put him where he is. You have to understand that and believe it. Meggie, I swear to you, on my mother's heart, that I will take you down there anytime you want to see him." She told him she wasn't sure she wanted to see him. "Then don't. You can call the nursing home too. Anytime you wish. You were given the name of his nurses and doctors. Call them. But don't let his being where he is eat you alive."

After thanking him for his help, she said she was going to go see Andonna. They had a meeting. Loman was happy about the meeting and knew that once she was in the other realm, she's be feeling much better. They just needed her to stay there for a few days and see if she could enjoy her life there. Meggie needed it. More than he thought when it was first brought up of her living there and being friends with Andonna.

He was headed to the building that he'd been told about that would make a great place for him to use as a base for his work. As he was entering the building, Amerdan joined him. She sat on his shoulder, and as soon as he opened the door, she went in ahead of him to turn on the lights. He fell in love with the place that quickly. He also heard from Lindsley.

"You've killed me." They both laughed. "I'm

getting into the shower, and I want to meet you where you are to hang out."

"I'm at the building that I'm going to be using for my home base for work. I think that it's the perfect setup." He found the room that he'd use for the dark room process. "I'm standing in the room I know was just made for me."

They talked for a bit longer then she told him that she was on her way. He remembered to tell her where her mom was and that Andi was at the pack house. Loman explained how he'd seen her on a dating app and told her to find a man around here.

"Good for you. She'll take your advice over mine every day of the week, I think." Again they laughed, and she said she was coming. He closed the connection and then asked Amerdan what she thought of the building.

"'Tis perfect for what I can see in your mind. The few things that need to be fixed, it won't take me but a moment." Before he could agree for her to make the changes, the place was just exactly how he'd envisioned it when he walked in the door. Christ, it was perfect. "I've made it so that there is a good lock on the door for you on the inside of the darkening room."

"Darkroom." Going into the room, he could see that there were already chemicals on shelves. That there was an enlarger, too, so that he could blow up the pictures that he liked. "This is wonderful, Amerdan. Thank you so much."

"My pleasure, my lord." When Lindsley arrived, he showed her what Amerdan had done for him. Not to be outdone in getting praise, Mitar cleaned the rest of the building up and even put in a place to take a break and eat. He was going to love having these two around, he thought.

~*~

The grand opening was in one hour. They had invited patrons of the arts and gallery to have a special showing last night. Six of his twenty pieces of art were already sold. He couldn't believe it. Also, the up-and-coming artist, a woman that did textile work, had several of her pieces sold as well. She was as excited as he was about how it was going.

"I've never been able to get my things out there. I'd heard so many horror stories about the gallery before that I wasn't ever going to come here. I'm so glad that you talked to me." He told her that he was happy that she'd agreed to come. "I can't thank you enough."

Her name was Doris Wickman, and she was a single mom with three children. Not only was this going to be a good income for her, but he had a feeling that it was going to be much more far-reaching than just this gallery.

When his family showed up, he could have hugged them all. They were dressed in tuxedos and long gowns. Even Lindsley was dressed in a beautiful gown that showed off every curve she had. Not to mention, the black sheath dress looked like it had been made just for her.

After the guests started to show, he was busy talking about one picture after the other. But always there at his side was Lindsley. She even encouraged him to tell the story of the tragic death of the calf that he'd decided to put into a series of pictures together.

"He couldn't have been more than a few days old." After telling the story, the man and woman walked away. "I guess it was too much for them. Should I have just softened it a little?"

"No. They asked for the story behind it, and I think that is what you should give them." They walked around, shaking hands with people he didn't know. Andi was in a man's suit, complete with a tie, and she looked like the part she was playing as a gallery owner. She kissed him on the cheek and thanked him for telling her about the pack.

"I have a date." They were all excited for her. "Jonah. We're going to go and see a movie, then he's taking me out to dinner. Isn't that wonderful? Also, you're not going to believe this, but he wants me to come around all the time. Even think about moving on the land."

"Andi, are you his mate?" She was so happy to share the news that Lindsley and her jumped for joy. They could be heard squealing around the entire gallery. When they calmed down, Lindsley asked her what she was going to do now. "I mean, you and him are mates. That's a big step for you and him. And he's the pack leader too."

"He explained things to me and told me that he'd been waiting for me for all his life. He's so romantic. And I just love being around him." Andi looked around. "Oh, I completely forgot what I was here to ask you, Loman. The couple that you were talking to, they wanted to know if you had any more pictures of the calf before he was killed. They have already purchased the set, but they want more to hang in their home."

"Yes. I have some really good shots of him with the tower. I'll send them to you right now. I'll have Amerdan send them to you. She's been a great help with things like this." He didn't even have to ask the fae to do it since she was with him all the time now. She heard his request and sent them on. The ringing of Andi's phone made him smile. "She's wonderfully helpful. I don't know what I'd do without her sometimes."

The couple bought three more pictures of the calf with the tower. He said he'd take care that they were the sizes they wanted and have them shipped to them. When walking around again after Andi went to talk to the couple, he saw that every one of his pictures had a sold sign on them. And Doris was making arrangements to have three of her art that had been sold duplicated so that she could get them to people that had wanted them too. He thought it was a highly successful evening for everyone.

"Tomorrow is the auction for the gems. Have you heard from the auctioneer about them?" He told Lindsley that he thought it would be an amazing sale. "Not that we need the money or anything, but I do hope he's right. Andi and I have great plans for that money in trying to make a difference in a lot of lives."

"I saw the list that Andi has. Those are some amazing causes that the two of you have in mind." She asked him if he'd help. "I will do whatever you wish for me to do to help you. I do have another shoot next week, but until then and after, I'm all yours."

"Did you know that when our fae are on our bodies, they can tell everything that is going on with us?" Loman told Lindsley that he figured at much. "Well, Mr. know it all, we're going to be parents."

"Great." He took a step forward, then stopped when what she said to him hit him. "I'm sorry, what did you say? We're going to have a baby?"

"Yes. In about seven months. Just in time for fall." He put his hand on her flat belly and looked at her. "Mitar said that if I wanted to know the sex, he could tell us. Even the day it will be born. I don't know that I'd want all that information right now. How about you?"

"No. I mean, yes. No. I'd like for it—are you really going to have a baby with me?" She nodded and put his hand on her heart. "I love you so much, Lindsley Foster. Thank you so much for giving me your heart."

"You've always had it, Loman. And now we're going to be able to share our love with a child that we created." On their way home, all they talked about was the baby. He was happier than he'd ever been.

Loman thought that he said that to himself a great deal. But he also knew that it was true. Every day was a better day. Each day with his family, all of them, was wonderful. And he knew that the future was going to be even better.

Getting ready to go on his shoot, he almost didn't want to leave. But he knew that if he didn't, he'd miss out on a great opportunity. This time he was shooting the wilds of the arctic tundra. He was excited about that.

Lindsley was going to be working on some of the things going on at the gallery, and she was also going to be setting up meetings with other artists. After the showing the night before, there were people all over the country that were wanting to be a part of what was going on. He was proud of all of them.

The flight he was taking was going to take him to a drop-off point then he was going to walk to the site where the polar bears were. He'd never been able to take pictures of bears in this setting as it was a dangerous place to be, and he couldn't get the permits needed to stay there.

Just as he was starting out on his journey, his cell phone rang. Seeing that it was the nursing home, he almost didn't want to answer it. When he did, he got the news that they'd all been expecting for some time. Allen had passed away peacefully in his sleep.

He thanked them for the call and asked after the arrangements. Meggie had donated his body to the college so that they could see the internal effects of the drug that he'd taken. Also, they were going to have him cremated once they were finished then Meggie would have the ashes. It was arrangements that he was happy for.

Calling Lindsley instead of reaching out to her, he told her about her father. She started crying, and his heart hurt for her. She asked him if he'd made sure that the arrangements were still in place.

"Yes. They told me what was on his file, and that is what Meggie and you guys wanted. His body is on its way to the college now, and they're going to take good care of him. Also, if you think it might help your mother, I'd tell her while she's in the other realm. There is a wonderful chance she will take it much better there than here." Lindsley said she loved that idea. "I don't know what to tell you about Andi. But I'd make sure that Jonah is with her. He'll be able to comfort her in ways that we can't."

"I agree with all of that. Yes, I'll take care of it on this end." She cried a bit more before telling him how much she loved him. "I just don't know what I'd do without you by my side."

"I have the same feelings for you, love." Loman wished he could be there with them, but he knew that Lindsley would be able to be strong for the family. As soon as he returned home from this trip, he was going to plan a long trip for the two of them. Get some things for the baby and have some fun. He had no idea if she had traveled much before meeting him, but it didn't matter, they were going to be together this time, and they'd make some wonderful memories.

It took him two days of walking to get to the place where he'd been told the bears were. He's spotted a few other animals on his way there and had been able to get some great shots of a snowy owl nesting. As well as a group of Arctic hares and foxes. When he was as close as he was going to get for the night, he was able to sit out in the twilight of the night and get more shots of the sun setting and the mountains of snow that he had never seen. By the time he was ready for bed, he'd taken over four hundred pictures.

While he was bedding down for the night, he lay outside of his small tent and watched the icebergs floating by. There were other animals around, some he had seen only in pictures. It was then that he spotted a mother polar bear and her cub.

Not moving, knowing that she'd attack him if he made a move toward her baby, he took several pictures of them playing around. It was more than he could have hoped for coming here. When he spotted the second cub, he nearly jumped up to get better pictures. Instead, he remained where he was and got a wonderful picture of the cubs playing with their mother.

He could have left then. He was so happy with his progress already. But tomorrow, he was going to be able to move a bit closer if there were no more bears around and see what he could find. When he realized that he was hungry and freezing, and just as he was thinking about it, he was warmer, and he had a few grapes in his lap. Thanking his fae for her help, he was almost afraid to pick one up and eat it. The momma bear finally noticed him.

He didn't move while sitting there. He knew that to run would get him mauled. When she started for him, he closed his eyes, fearful of seeing her large paws slashing him. When one of the cubs sat in his lap, he nearly laughed. But he watched the momma, who unbelievably sat down beside him. It was then that he noticed that she'd been hurt. Badly too.

The arrow that was in her shoulder had been broken off. When he put his hand over the area, he watched as it seemed to be healing up. As soon as the arrowhead fell on the snow, bloodied and sharp, Loman put his hand over the wound and thought about her being healed.

"She knows that you are fae." Asking Amerdan if he was fae or it was her, she laughed a little. "Nay, you are fae. I am just here to make sure that she doesn't harm you. I don't believe that she will, but you must be careful."

He said that he would. The second cub came to play in his lap, and he wished that he'd set up his remote cameras so that he could get shots of this interaction. They were eating his grapes and having fun. Amerdan made sure that there was more for them to munch on while their mother rested. Loman was careful not to get too attached to the little bear, but it was hard. They were so cute that he couldn't resist playing with them too.

"I have taken shots, as you call them, of the play here, my lord." He asked her how she'd done that. "I'm magical."

He figured that was all he was going to get from her and let it go. Just as the sun was coming up, momma bear sat up. The little ones came to her, and again Amerdan surprised him. She made sure there were fish and other fresh sea creatures there for the big bear to eat. The cubs, still small, joined their momma while she tore into the food like she'd not eaten in some time.

"It has been difficult for her to care for her cubs and hunt with the wound in her shoulder. If you had not come along when you had, she would have perished, and the cubs would have too. I know that you're not to interfere with nature, but the cubs will go on to have several cubs of their own now and help with the population of the polar bear population." He thanked her again. "You are a good man, my lord. I do hope that you remember that for the rest of your life. A good man you are, and I am honored to work with you."

He was humbled by her words. It wasn't often that he was able to be rendered speechless from someone. But it felt good to be able to be a part of her life as well.

Once momma bear was well enough to move on, she licked him on the face and took off running. The cubs following her. Wherever they were going, he was sure that they'd be safe now.

Crawling into his tent, he looked at the photos that Amerdan had taken for him. They were excellent.

Not that he'd be able to show anyone some of them, but he would show them to his family so that they could get a kick out of the cubs. He was ready to go home now to do it, but he had to get some pictures that he could sell. Life was good, he thought again and again. Better than he could have expected even a year ago.

Epilogue:

This isn't the end of the Foster story. It's only the beginning of a wonderful story. They're going to be helpful in a great many pride's lives, starting with the Tucker family. My goodness, there are a lot of them to help too.

The Tucker family is coming soon, I think. They will lean heavily on the Fosters at the start. The king and queen are more than happy to help them. The Tucker's will be a wonderful pride and a happy family.

Do you think they'll all find wonderful mates too? Hard to tell. You'll just have to wait and see with me. I think Muse had great plans for the Tuckers, and we'll share them with you soon.

June brides and mates sound good to me. What do you think?

Before You Go...

HELP AN AUTHOR

write a review

THANK YOU!

Share your voice and help guide other readers to these wonderful books. Even if it's only a line or two, your reviews help readers discover the author's books so they can continue creating stories that you'll love. Log in to your favorite retailer and leave a review. Thank you.

AWARD WINNING, BESTSELLING AUTHOR

Kathi Barton, a winner of the Pinnacle Book Achievement Award and a best-selling author on Amazon and All Romance books, lives in Nashport, Ohio, with her husband, Paul. When not creating new worlds and romance, Kathi and her husband enjoy camping and going to auctions. She can also be seen at county fairs with her husband, an artist and potter.

Her muse, a cross between Jimmy Stewart and Hugh Jackman, brings her stories to life for her readers in a way that has them coming back time and again for more. Her favorite genre is paranormal romance, with a great deal of spice. You can visit Kathi online and drop her an email if you'd like. She loves hearing from her fans. aaronskiss@gmail.com.

Follow Kathi on her blog: http://kathisbartonauthor.blogspot.com/

www.ingramcontent.com/pod-product-compliance
Lightning Source LLC
Chambersburg PA
CBHW020123180626
46810CB00014B/2917